The Sarah, Plain and Tall Treasury

Patricia MacLachlan

Including:

Sarah, Plain and Tall

Skylark

Caleb's Story

BARNES
&NOBLE
BOOKS

The Sarah, Plain and Tall Treasury:
Sarah, Plain and Tall
Skylark
Caleb's Story

A Barnes&Noble Books edition, published by permission of
HarperCollins Children's Books

Printed in the United States of America. For information address HarperCollins Children's Books, a division of HarperCollins Publishers, 1350 Avenue of the Americas, New York, NY 10019.
www.harperchildrens.com
www.bn.com

Patricia MacLachlan

Sarah, Plain and Tall

For old friends, dear friends—

DICK AND WENDY PUFF,

ALLISON AND DEREK

Sarah, Plain and Tall

I

"Did Mama sing every day?" asked Caleb. "Every-single-day?" He sat close to the fire, his chin in his hand. It was dusk, and the dogs lay beside him on the warm hearthstones.

"Every-single-day," I told him for the second time this week. For the twentieth time this month. The hundredth time this year? And the past few years?

"And did Papa sing, too?"

"Yes. Papa sang, too. Don't get so close, Caleb. You'll heat up."

He pushed his chair back. It made a hollow scraping sound on the hearthstones, and the dogs stirred. Lottie, small and black, wagged her tail and lifted her head. Nick slept on.

4

I turned the bread dough over and over on the marble slab on the kitchen table.

"Well, Papa doesn't sing anymore," said Caleb very softly. A log broke apart and crackled in the fireplace. He looked up at me. "What did I look like when I was born?"

"You didn't have any clothes on," I told him.

"I know that," he said.

"You looked like this." I held the bread dough up in a round pale ball.

"I had hair," said Caleb seriously.

"Not enough to talk about," I said.

"And she named me Caleb," he went on, filling in the old familiar story.

"*I* would have named you Troublesome," I said, making Caleb smile.

"And Mama handed me to you in the yellow blanket and said . . ." He waited for me to finish the story. "And said . . . ?"

I sighed. "And Mama said, 'Isn't he beautiful, Anna?' "

"And I was," Caleb finished.

Caleb thought the story was over, and I didn't

tell him what I had really thought. He was homely and plain, and he had a terrible holler and a horrid smell. But these were not the worst of him. Mama died the next morning. That was the worst thing about Caleb.

"Isn't he beautiful, Anna?" Her last words to me. I had gone to bed thinking how wretched he looked. And I forgot to say good night.

I wiped my hands on my apron and went to the window. Outside, the prairie reached out and touched the places where the sky came down. Though winter was nearly over, there were patches of snow and ice everywhere. I looked at the long dirt road that crawled across the plains, remembering the morning that Mama had died, cruel and sunny. They had come for her in a wagon and taken her away to be buried. And then the cousins and aunts and uncles had come and tried to fill up the house. But they couldn't.

Slowly, one by one, they left. And then the days seemed long and dark like winter days, even though it wasn't winter. And Papa didn't sing.

6

Isn't he beautiful, Anna?

No, Mama.

It was hard to think of Caleb as beautiful. It took three whole days for me to love him, sitting in the chair by the fire, Papa washing up the supper dishes, Caleb's tiny hand brushing my cheek. And a smile. It was the smile, I know.

"Can you remember her songs?" asked Caleb. "Mama's songs?"

I turned from the window. "No. Only that she sang about flowers and birds. Sometimes about the moon at nighttime."

Caleb reached down and touched Lottie's head.

"Maybe," he said, his voice low, "if you remember the songs, then I might remember her, too."

My eyes widened and tears came. Then the door opened and wind blew in with Papa, and I went to stir the stew. Papa put his arms around me and put his nose in my hair.

"Nice soapy smell, that stew," he said.

I laughed. "That's my hair "

Caleb came over and threw his arms around

Papa's neck and hung down as Papa swung him back and forth, and the dogs sat up.

"Cold in town," said Papa. "And Jack was feisty." Jack was Papa's horse that he'd raised from a colt. "Rascal," murmured Papa, smiling, because no matter what Jack did Papa loved him.

I spooned up the stew and lighted the oil lamp and we ate with the dogs crowding under the table, hoping for spills or handouts.

Papa might not have told us about Sarah that night if Caleb hadn't asked him the question. After the dishes were cleared and washed and Papa was filling the tin pail with ashes, Caleb spoke up. It wasn't a question, really.

"You don't sing anymore," he said. He said it harshly. Not because he meant to, but because he had been thinking of it for so long. "Why?" he asked more gently.

Slowly Papa straightened up. There was a long silence, and the dogs looked up, wondering at it.

"I've forgotten the old songs," said Papa quietly. He sat down. "But maybe there's a way to remember them." He looked up at us.

"How?" asked Caleb eagerly.

8

Papa leaned back in the chair. "I've placed an advertisement in the newspapers. For help."

"You mean a housekeeper?" I asked, surprised.

Caleb and I looked at each other and burst out laughing, remembering Hilly, our old housekeeper. She was round and slow and shuffling. She snored in a high whistle at night, like a teakettle, and let the fire go out.

"No," said Papa slowly. "Not a housekeeper." He paused. "A wife."

Caleb stared at Papa. "A wife? You mean a mother?"

Nick slid his face onto Papa's lap and Papa stroked his ears.

"That, too," said Papa. "Like Maggie."

Matthew, our neighbor to the south, had written to ask for a wife and mother for his children. And Maggie had come from Tennessee. Her hair was the color of turnips and she laughed.

Papa reached into his pocket and unfolded a letter written on white paper. "And I have received an answer." Papa read to us:

"Dear Mr. Jacob Witting,

"I am Sarah Wheaton from Maine as you will see from my letter. I am answering your advertisement. I have never been married, though I have been asked. I have lived with an older brother, William, who is about to be married. His wife-to-be is young and energetic.

"I have always loved to live by the sea, but at this time I feel a move is necessary. And the truth is, the sea is as far east as I can go. My choice, as you can see, is limited. This should not be taken as an insult. I am strong and I work hard and I am willing to travel. But I am not mild mannered. If you should still care to write, I would be interested in your children and about where you live. And you.

"Very truly yours,
"Sarah Elisabeth Wheaton

"P.S. Do you have opinions on cats? I have one."

No one spoke when Papa finished the letter. He kept looking at it in his hands, reading it over to himself. Finally I turned my head a bit to sneak a look at Caleb. He was smiling. I smiled, too.

"One thing," I said in the quiet of the room.

"What's that?" asked Papa, looking up.

I put my arm around Caleb.

"Ask her if she sings," I said.

2

Caleb and Papa and I wrote letters to Sarah, and before the ice and snow had melted from the fields, we all received answers. Mine came first.

Dear Anna,

Yes, I can braid hair and I can make stew and bake bread, though I prefer to build bookshelves and paint.

My favorite colors are the colors of the sea, blue and gray and green, depending on the weather. My brother William is a fisherman, and he tells me that when he is in the middle of a fog-bound sea the water is a color for which there is no name. He catches flounder and sea bass and bluefish. Sometimes he sees whales. And birds, too, of course. I am enclosing a book of sea birds so you will see what William and I see every day.

Very truly yours,
Sarah Elisabeth Wheaton

Caleb read and read the letter so many times that the ink began to run and the folds tore. He read the book about sea birds over and over.

"Do you think she'll come?" asked Caleb. "And will she stay? What if she thinks we are loud and pesky?"

"You *are* loud and pesky," I told him. But I was worried, too. Sarah loved the sea, I could tell. Maybe she wouldn't leave there after all to come where there were fields and grass and sky and not much else.

"What if she comes and doesn't like our house?" Caleb asked. "I told her it was small. Maybe I shouldn't have told her it was small."

"Hush, Caleb. Hush."

Caleb's letter came soon after, with a picture of a cat drawn on the envelope.

Dear Caleb,

My cat's name is Seal because she is gray like the seals that swim offshore in Maine. She is glad that Lottie and Nick send their greetings. She likes dogs most of the time. She says their footprints are much larger than hers (which she is enclosing in return).

Your house sounds lovely, even though it is far out in the country with no close neighbors. My house is tall and the shingles are gray because of the salt from the sea. There are roses nearby.

Yes, I do like small rooms sometimes. Yes, I can keep a fire going at night. I do not know if I snore. Seal has never told me.

Very truly yours,
Sarah Elisabeth

"Did you really ask her about fires and snoring?" I asked, amazed.

"I wished to know," Caleb said.

He kept the letter with him, reading it in the barn and in the fields and by the cow pond. And always in bed at night.

14

One morning, early, Papa and Caleb and I were cleaning out the horse stalls and putting down new bedding. Papa stopped suddenly and leaned on his pitchfork.

"Sarah has said she will come for a month's time if we wish her to," he said, his voice loud in the dark barn. "To see how it is. Just to see."

Caleb stood by the stall door and folded his arms across his chest.

"I think," he began. Then, "I think," he said slowly, "that it would be good—to say yes," he finished in a rush.

Papa looked at me.

"I say yes," I told him, grinning.

"Yes," said Papa. "Then yes it is."

And the three of us, all smiling, went to work again.

The next day Papa went to town to mail his letter to Sarah. It was rainy for days, and the clouds followed. The house was cool and damp and quiet. Once I set four places at the table, then caught myself and put the extra plate away. Three lambs were born, one with a black face. And then Papa's letter came. It was very short.

Dear Jacob,

I will come by train. I will wear a yellow bonnet. I am plain and tall.

Sarah

"What's that?" asked Caleb excitedly, peering over Papa's shoulder. He pointed. "There, written at the bottom of the letter."

Papa read it to himself. Then he smiled, holding up the letter for us to see.

Tell them I sing was all it said.

3

Sarah came in the spring. She came through green grass fields that bloomed with Indian paintbrush, red and orange, and blue-eyed grass.

Papa got up early for the long day's trip to the train and back. He brushed his hair so slick and shiny that Caleb laughed. He wore a clean blue shirt, and a belt instead of suspenders.

He fed and watered the horses, talking to them as he hitched them up to the wagon. Old Bess, calm and kind; Jack, wild-eyed, reaching over to nip Bess on the neck.

"Clear day, Bess," said Papa, rubbing her nose.

"Settle down, Jack." He leaned his head on Jack.

And then Papa drove off along the dirt road

to fetch Sarah. Papa's new wife. Maybe. Maybe our new mother.

Gophers ran back and forth across the road, stopping to stand up and watch the wagon. Far off in the field a woodchuck ate and listened. Ate and listened.

Caleb and I did our chores without talking. We shoveled out the stalls and laid down new hay. We fed the sheep. We swept and straightened and carried wood and water. And then our chores were done.

Caleb pulled on my shirt.

"Is my face clean?" he asked. "Can my face be *too* clean?" He looked alarmed.

"No, your face is clean but not too clean," I said.

Caleb slipped his hand into mine as we stood on the porch, watching the road. He was afraid.

"Will she be nice?" he asked. "Like Maggie?"

"Sarah will be nice," I told him.

"How far away is Maine?" he asked.

"You know how far. Far away, by the sea."

"Will Sarah bring some sea?" he asked.

"No, you cannot bring the sea."

The sheep ran in the field, and far off the cows moved slowly to the pond, like turtles.

"Will she like us?" asked Caleb very softly.

I watched a marsh hawk wheel down behind the barn.

He looked up at me.

"Of course she will like us." He answered his own question. "We are nice," he added, making me smile.

We waited and watched. I rocked on the porch and Caleb rolled a marble on the wood floor. Back and forth. Back and forth. The marble was blue.

We saw the dust from the wagon first, rising above the road, above the heads of Jack and Old Bess. Caleb climbed up onto the porch roof and shaded his eyes.

"A bonnet!" he cried. "I see a yellow bonnet!"

The dogs came out from under the porch, ears up, their eyes on the cloud of dust bringing Sarah. The wagon passed the fenced field, and the cows and sheep looked up, too. It rounded the windmill and the barn and the windbreak of

Russian olive that Mama had planted long ago. Nick began to bark, then Lottie, and the wagon clattered into the yard and stopped by the steps.

"Hush," said Papa to the dogs.

And it was quiet.

Sarah stepped down from the wagon, a cloth bag in her hand. She reached up and took off her yellow bonnet, smoothing back her brown hair into a bun. She was plain and tall.

"Did you bring some sea?" cried Caleb beside me.

"Something from the sea," said Sarah, smiling. "And me." She turned and lifted a black case from the wagon. "And Seal, too."

Carefully she opened the case, and Seal, gray with white feet, stepped out. Lottie lay down, her head on her paws, staring. Nick leaned down to sniff. Then he lay down, too.

"The cat will be good in the barn," said Papa. "For mice."

Sarah smiled. "She will be good in the house, too."

Sarah took Caleb's hand, then mine. Her hands were large and rough. She gave Caleb a shell—

a moon snail, she called it—that was curled and smelled of salt.

"The gulls fly high and drop the shells on the rocks below," she told Caleb. "When the shell is broken, they eat what is inside."

"That is very smart," said Caleb.

"For you, Anna," said Sarah, "a sea stone."

And she gave me the smoothest and whitest stone I had ever seen.

"The sea washes over and over and around the stone, rolling it until it is round and perfect."

"That is very smart, too," said Caleb. He looked up at Sarah. "We do not have the sea here."

Sarah turned and looked out over the plains. "No," she said. "There is no sea here. But the land rolls a little like the sea."

My father did not see her look, but I did. And I knew that Caleb had seen it, too. Sarah was not smiling. Sarah was already lonely. In a month's time the preacher might come to marry Sarah and Papa. And a month was a long time. Time enough for her to change her mind and leave us.

Papa took Sarah's bags inside, where her room

was ready with a quilt on the bed and blue flax dried in a vase on the night table.

Seal stretched and made a small cat sound. I watched her circle the dogs and sniff the air. Caleb came out and stood beside me.

"When will we sing?" he whispered.

I shook my head, turning the white stone over and over in my hand. I wished everything was as perfect as the stone. I wished that Papa and Caleb and I were perfect for Sarah. I wished we had a sea of our own.

4

The dogs loved Sarah first. Lottie slept beside her bed, curled in a soft circle, and Nick leaned his face on the covers in the morning, watching for the first sign that Sarah was awake. No one knew where Seal slept. Seal was a roamer.

Sarah's collection of shells sat on the window-sill.

"A scallop," she told us, picking up the shells one by one, "a sea clam, an oyster, a razor clam. And a conch shell. If you put it to your ear you can hear the sea." She put it to Caleb's ear, then mine. Papa listened, too. Then Sarah listened once more, with a look so sad and far away that Caleb leaned against me.

"At least Sarah can hear the sea," he whispered.

Papa was quiet and shy with Sarah, and so was I. But Caleb talked to Sarah from morning until the light left the sky.

"Where are you going?" he asked. "To do what?"

"To pick flowers," said Sarah. "I'll hang some of them upside down and dry them so they'll keep some color. And we can have flowers all winter long."

"I'll come, too!" cried Caleb. "Sarah said winter," he said to me. "That means Sarah will stay."

Together we picked flowers, paintbrush and clover and prairie violets. There were buds on the wild roses that climbed up the paddock fence.

"The roses will bloom in early summer," I told Sarah. I looked to see if she knew what I was thinking. Summer was when the wedding would be. *Might* be. Sarah and Papa's wedding.

We hung the flowers from the ceiling in little bunches. "I've never seen this before," said Sarah. "What is it called?"

"Bride's bonnet," I told her.

Caleb smiled at the name.

"We don't have this by the sea," she said. "We have seaside goldenrod and wild asters and woolly ragwort."

"Woolly ragwort!" Caleb whooped. He made up a song.

"Woolly ragwort all around,
Woolly ragwort on the ground.
Woolly ragwort grows and grows,
Woolly ragwort in your nose."

Sarah and Papa laughed, and the dogs lifted their heads and thumped their tails against the wood floor. Seal sat on a kitchen chair and watched us with yellow eyes.

We ate Sarah's stew, the late light coming through the windows. Papa had baked bread that was still warm from the fire.

"The stew is fine," said Papa.

"Ayuh." Sarah nodded. "The bread, too."

"What does 'ayuh' mean?" asked Caleb.

"In Maine it means yes," said Sarah. "Do you want more stew?"

"Ayuh," said Caleb.

"Ayuh," echoed my father.

After dinner Sarah told us about William. "He has a gray-and-white boat named *Kittiwake*." She looked out the window. "That is a small gull found way off the shore where William fishes. There are three aunts who live near us. They wear silk dresses and no shoes. You would love them."

"Ayuh," said Caleb.

"Does your brother look like you?" I asked.

"Yes," said Sarah. "He is plain and tall."

At dusk Sarah cut Caleb's hair on the front steps, gathering his curls and scattering them on the fence and ground. Seal batted some hair around the porch as the dogs watched.

"Why?" asked Caleb.

"For the birds," said Sarah. "They will use it for their nests. Later we can look for nests of curls."

"Sarah said 'later,' " Caleb whispered to me as we spread his hair about. "Sarah will stay."

Sarah cut Papa's hair, too. No one else saw, but I found him behind the barn, tossing the pieces of hair into the wind for the birds.

Sarah brushed my hair and tied it up in back

with a rose velvet ribbon she had brought from Maine. She brushed hers long and free and tied it back, too, and we stood side by side looking into the mirror. I looked taller, like Sarah, and fair and thin. And with my hair pulled back I looked a little like her daughter. Sarah's daughter.

And then it was time for singing.

Sarah sang us a song we had never heard before as we sat on the porch, insects buzzing in the dark, the rustle of cows in the grasses. It was called "Sumer Is Icumen in," and she taught it to us all, even Papa, who sang as if he had never stopped singing.

> *"Sumer is icumen in,*
> *Lhude sing cuccu!"*

"What is sumer?" asked Caleb. He said it "soomer," the way Sarah had said it.

"Summer," said Papa and Sarah at the same time. Caleb and I looked at each other. Summer was coming.

"Tomorrow," said Sarah, "I want to see the sheep. You know, I've never touched one."

"Never?" Caleb sat up.

"Never," said Sarah. She smiled and leaned back in her chair. "But I've touched seals. Real seals. They are cool and slippery and they slide through the water like fish. They can cry and sing. And sometimes they bark, a little like dogs."

Sarah barked like a seal. And Lottie and Nick came running from the barn to jump up on Sarah and lick her face and make her laugh. Sarah stroked them and scratched their ears and it was quiet again.

"I wish I could touch a seal right now," said Caleb, his voice soft in the night.

"So do I," said Sarah. She sighed, then she began to sing the summer song again. Far off in a field, a meadowlark sang, too.

5

The sheep made Sarah smile. She sank her fingers into their thick, coarse wool. She talked to them, running with the lambs, letting them suck on her fingers. She named them after her favorite aunts, Harriet and Mattie and Lou. She lay down in the field beside them and sang "Sumer Is Icumen in," her voice drifting over the meadow grasses, carried by the wind.

She cried when we found a lamb that had died, and she shouted and shook her fist at the turkey buzzards that came from nowhere to eat it. She would not let Caleb or me come near. And that night, Papa went with a shovel to bury the sheep and a lantern to bring Sarah back. She sat on the porch alone. Nick crept up to lean against her knees.

After dinner, Sarah drew pictures to send home to Maine. She began a charcoal drawing of the fields, rolling like the sea rolled. She drew a sheep whose ears were too big. And she drew a windmill.

"Windmill was my first word," said Caleb. "Papa told me so."

"Mine was flower," I said. "What was yours, Sarah?"

"Dune," said Sarah.

"Dune?" Caleb looked up.

"In Maine," said Sarah, "there are rock cliffs that rise up at the edge of the sea. And there are hills covered with pine and spruce trees, green with needles. But William and I found a sand dune all our own. It was soft and sparkling with bits of mica, and when we were little we would slide down the dune into the water."

Caleb looked out the window.

"We have no dunes here," he said.

Papa stood up.

"Yes we do," he said. He took the lantern and went out the door to the barn.

"We do?" Caleb called after him.

He ran ahead, Sarah and I following, the dogs close behind.

Next to the barn was Papa's mound of hay for bedding, nearly half as tall as the barn, covered with canvas to keep the rain from rotting it. Papa carried the wooden ladder from the barn and leaned it against the hay.

"There." He smiled at Sarah. "Our dune."

Sarah was very quiet. The dogs looked up at her, waiting. Seal brushed against her legs, her tail in the air. Caleb reached over and took her hand.

"It looks high up," he said. "Are you scared, Sarah?"

"Scared? Scared!" exclaimed Sarah. "You bet I'm not scared."

She climbed the ladder, and Nick began to bark. She climbed to the very top of the hay and sat, looking down at us. Above, the stars were coming out. Papa piled a bed of loose hay below with his pitchfork. The light of the lantern made his eyes shine when he smiled up at Sarah.

"Fine?" called Papa.

"Fine," said Sarah. She lifted her arms over her head and slid down, down, into the soft hay. She lay, laughing, as the dogs rolled beside her.

"Was it a good dune?" called Caleb.

"Yes," said Sarah. "It is a fine dune."

Caleb and I climbed up and slid down. And Sarah did it three more times. At last Papa slid down, too, as the sky grew darker and the stars blinked like fireflies. We were covered with hay and dust, and we sneezed.

In the kitchen, Caleb and I washed in the big wooden tub and Sarah drew more pictures to send to William. One was of Papa, his hair curly and full of hay. She drew Caleb, sliding down the hay, his arms like Sarah's over his head. And she drew a picture of me in the tub, my hair long and straight and wet. She looked at her drawing of the fields for a long time.

"Something is missing," she told Caleb. "Something." And she put it away.

" 'Dear William,' " Sarah read to us by lantern light that night. " 'Sliding down our dune of hay is almost as fine as sliding down the sand dunes into the sea.' "

Caleb smiled at me across the table. He said nothing, but his mouth formed the words I had heard, too. *Our dune.*

6

The days grew longer. The cows moved close to the pond, where the water was cool and there were trees.

Papa taught Sarah how to plow the fields, guiding the plow behind Jack and Old Bess, the reins around her neck. When the chores were done we sat in the meadow with the sheep, Sarah beside us, watching Papa finish.

"Tell me about winter," said Sarah.

Old Bess nodded her head as she walked, but we could hear Papa speak sharply to Jack.

"Jack doesn't like work," said Caleb. "He wants to be here in the sweet grass with us."

"I don't blame him," said Sarah. She lay back in the grass with her arms under her head. "Tell me about winter," she said again.

"Winter is cold here," said Caleb, and Sarah and I laughed.

"Winter is cold everywhere," I said.

"We go to school in winter," said Caleb. "Sums and writing and books," he sang.

"I am good at sums and writing," said Sarah. "I love books. How do you get to school?"

"Papa drives us in the wagon. Or we walk the three miles when there is not too much snow."

Sarah sat up. "Do you have lots of snow?"

"Lots and lots and lots of snow," chanted Caleb, rolling around in the grass. "Sometimes we have to dig our way out to feed the animals."

"In Maine the barns are attached to the houses sometimes," said Sarah.

Caleb grinned. "So you could have a cow to Sunday supper?"

Sarah and I laughed.

"When there are bad storms, Papa ties a rope from the house to the barn so no one will get lost," said Caleb.

I frowned. I loved winter.

"There is ice on the windows on winter mornings," I told Sarah. "We can draw sparkling pictures and we can see our breath in the air. Papa builds a warm fire, and we bake hot biscuits and put on hundreds of sweaters. And if the snow is too high, we stay home from school and make snow people."

Sarah lay back in the tall grasses again, her face nearly hidden.

"And is there wind?" she asked.

"Do you like wind?" asked Caleb.

"There is wind by the sea," said Sarah.

"There is wind here," said Caleb happily. "It blows the snow and brings tumbleweeds and makes the sheep run. Wind and wind and wind!" Caleb stood up and ran like the wind, and the sheep ran after him. Sarah and I watched him jump over rock and gullies, the sheep behind him, stiff legged and fast. He circled the field, the sun making the top of his hair golden. He collapsed next to Sarah, and the lambs pushed their wet noses into us.

"Hello, Lou," said Sarah, smiling. "Hello, Mattie."

The sun rose higher, and Papa stopped to take off his hat and wipe his face with his sleeve.

"I'm hot," said Sarah. "I can't wait for winter wind. Let's swim."

"Swim where?" I asked her.

"I can't swim," said Caleb.

"Can't swim!" exclaimed Sarah. "I'll teach you in the cow pond."

"That's for cows!" I cried.

But Sarah had grabbed our hands and we were running through the fields, ducking under the fence to the far pond.

"Shoo, cows," said Sarah as the cows looked up, startled. She took off her dress and waded into the water in her petticoat. She dived suddenly and disappeared for a moment as Caleb and I watched. She came up, laughing, her hair streaming free. Water beads sat on her shoulders.

She tried to teach us how to float. I sank like a bucket filled with water and came up sputtering. But Caleb lay on his back and learned how to blow streams of water high in the air like a whale. The cows stood on the banks of the pond and stared and stopped their chewing. Water bugs circled us.

"Is this like the sea?" asked Caleb.

Sarah treaded water.

"The sea is salt," said Sarah. "It stretches out as far as you can see. It gleams like the sun on glass. There are waves."

"Like this?" asked Caleb, and he pushed a wave at Sarah, making her cough and laugh.

"Yes," she said. "Like that."

I held my breath and floated at last, looking up into the sky, afraid to speak. Crows flew over, three in a row. And I could hear a killdeer in the field.

We climbed the bank and dried ourselves and lay in the grass again. The cows watched, their eyes sad in their dinner-plate faces. And I slept, dreaming a perfect dream. The fields had turned to a sea that gleamed like sun on glass. And Sarah was happy.

7

The dandelions in the fields had gone by, their heads soft as feathers. The summer roses were opening.

Our neighbors, Matthew and Maggie, came to help Papa plow up a new field for corn. Sarah stood with us on the porch, watching their wagon wind up the road, two horses pulling it and one tied in back. I remembered the last time we had stood here alone, Caleb and I, waiting for Sarah.

Sarah's hair was in thick braids that circled her head, wild daisies tucked here and there. Papa had picked them for her.

Old Bess and Jack ran along the inside of the fence, whickering at the new horses.

"Papa needs five horses for the big gang plow," Caleb told Sarah. "Prairie grass is hard."

Matthew and Maggie came with their two children and a sackful of chickens. Maggie emptied the sack into the yard and three red banty chickens clucked and scattered.

"They are for you," she told Sarah. "For eating."

Sarah loved the chickens. She clucked back to them and fed them grain. They followed her, shuffling and scratching primly in the dirt. I knew they would not be for eating.

The children were young and named Rose and Violet, after flowers. They hooted and laughed and chased the chickens, who flew up to the porch roof, then the dogs, who crept quietly under the porch. Seal had long ago fled to the barn to sleep in cool hay.

Sarah and Maggie helped hitch the horses to the plow, then they set up a big table in the shade of the barn, covering it with a quilt and a kettle of flowers in the middle. They sat on the porch while Caleb and Matthew and Papa began their morning of plowing. I mixed biscuit dough just inside the door, watching.

"You are lonely, yes?" asked Maggie in her soft voice.

Sarah's eyes filled with tears. Slowly I stirred the dough.

Maggie reached over and took Sarah's hand.

"I miss the hills of Tennessee sometimes," she said.

Do not miss the hills, Maggie, I thought.

"I miss the sea," said Sarah.

Do not miss the hills. Do not miss the sea.

I stirred and stirred the dough.

"I miss my brother William," said Sarah. "But he is married. The house is hers now. Not mine any longer. There are three old aunts who all squawk together like crows at dawn. I miss them, too."

"There are always things to miss," said Maggie. "No matter where you are."

I looked out and saw Papa and Matthew and Caleb working. Rose and Violet ran in the fields. I felt something brush my legs and looked down at Nick, wagging his tail.

"I would miss you, Nick," I whispered. "I would." I knelt down and scratched his ears. "I miss Mama."

"I nearly forgot," said Maggie on the porch. "I have something more for you."

I carried the bowl outside and watched Maggie lift a low wooden box out of the wagon.

"Plants," she said to Sarah. "For your garden."

"My garden?" Sarah bent down to touch the plants.

"Zinnias and marigolds and wild feverfew," said Maggie. "You must have a garden. Wherever you are."

Sarah smiled. "I had a garden in Maine with dahlias and columbine. And nasturtiums the color of the sun when it sets. I don't know if nasturtiums would grow here."

"Try," said Maggie. "You must have a garden."

We planted the flowers by the porch, turning over the soil and patting it around them, and watering. Lottie and Nick came to sniff, and the chickens walked in the dirt, leaving prints.

In the fields, the horses pulled the plow up and down under the hot summer sun.

Maggie wiped her face, leaving a streak of dirt.

"Soon you can drive your wagon over to my house and I will give you more. I have tansy."

Sarah frowned. "I have never driven a wagon."

"I can teach you," said Maggie. "And so can Anna and Caleb. And Jacob."

Sarah turned to me.

"Can you?" she asked. "Can you drive a wagon?"

I nodded.

"And Caleb?"

"Yes."

"In Maine," said Sarah, "I would walk to town."

"Here it is different," said Maggie. "Here you will drive."

Way off in the sky, clouds gathered. Matthew and Papa and Caleb came in from the fields, their work done. We all ate in the shade.

"We are glad you are here," said Matthew to

Sarah. "A new friend. Maggie misses her friends sometimes."

Sarah nodded. "There is always something to miss, no matter where you are," she said, smiling at Maggie.

Rose and Violet fell asleep in the grass, their bellies full of meat and greens and biscuits. And when it was time to go, Papa and Matthew lifted them into the wagon to sleep on blankets.

Sarah walked slowly behind the wagon for a long time, waving, watching it disappear. Caleb and I ran to bring her back, the chickens running wildly behind us.

"What shall we name them?" asked Sarah, laughing as the chickens followed us into the house.

I smiled. I was right. The chickens would not be for eating.

And then Papa came, just before the rain, bringing Sarah the first roses of summer.

8

The rain came and passed, but strange clouds hung in the northwest, low and black and green. And the air grew still.

In the morning, Sarah dressed in a pair of overalls and went to the barn to have an argument with Papa. She took apples for Old Bess and Jack.

"Women don't wear overalls," said Caleb, running along behind her like one of Sarah's chickens.

"This woman does," said Sarah crisply.

Papa stood by the fence.

"I want to learn how to ride a horse," Sarah told him. "And then I want to learn how to drive the wagon. By myself."

Jack leaned over and nipped at Sarah's overalls. She fed him an apple. Caleb and I stood behind Sarah.

"I can ride a horse, I know," said Sarah. "I rode once when I was twelve. I will ride Jack." Jack was Sarah's favorite.

Papa shook his head. "Not Jack," he said. "Jack is sly."

"I am sly, too," said Sarah stubbornly.

Papa smiled. "Ayuh," he said, nodding. "But not Jack."

"Yes, Jack!" Sarah's voice was very loud.

"I can teach you how to drive a wagon. I have already taught you how to plow."

"And then I can go to town. By myself."

"Say no, Papa," Caleb whispered beside me.

"That's a fair thing, Sarah," said Papa. "We'll practice."

A soft rumble of thunder sounded. Papa looked up at the clouds.

"Today? Can we begin today?" asked Sarah.

"Tomorrow is best," said Papa, looking worried. "I have to fix the house roof. A portion of it is loose. And there's a storm coming."

"We," said Sarah.

"What?" Papa turned.

"*We* will fix the roof," said Sarah. "I've done it before. I know about roofs. I am a good carpenter. Remember, I told you?"

There was thunder again, and Papa went to get the ladder.

"Are you fast?" he asked Sarah.

"I am fast and I am good," said Sarah. And they climbed the ladder to the roof, Sarah with wisps of hair around her face, her mouth full of nails, overalls like Papa's. Overalls that *were* Papa's.

Caleb and I went inside to close the windows. We could hear the steady sound of hammers pounding the roof overhead.

"Why does she want to go to town by herself?" asked Caleb. "To leave us?"

I shook my head, weary with Caleb's questions. Tears gathered at the corners of my eyes. But there was no time to cry, for suddenly Papa called out.

"Caleb! Anna!"

We ran outside and saw a huge cloud, horribly

black, moving toward us over the north fields. Papa slid down the roof, helping Sarah after him.

"A squall!" he yelled to us. He held up his arms and Sarah jumped off the porch roof.

"Get the horses inside," he ordered Caleb. "Get the sheep, Anna. And the cows. The barn is safest."

The grasses flattened. There was a hiss of wind, a sudden pungent smell. Our faces looked yellow in the strange light. Caleb and I jumped over the fence and found the animals huddled by the barn. I counted the sheep to make sure they were all there, and herded them into a large stall. A few raindrops came, gentle at first, then stronger and louder, so that Caleb and I covered our ears and stared at each other without speaking. Caleb looked frightened and I tried to smile at him. Sarah carried a sack into the barn, her hair wet and streaming down her neck, Papa came behind, Lottie and Nick with him, their ears flat against their heads.

"Wait!" cried Sarah. "My chickens!"

"No, Sarah!" Papa called after her. But Sarah had already run from the barn into a sheet of rain. My father followed her. The sheep nosed open their stall door and milled around the barn, bleating. Nick crept under my arm, and a lamb, Mattie with the black face, stood close to me, trembling. There was a soft paw on my lap, then a gray body. Seal. And then, as the thunder pounded and the wind rose and there was the terrible crackling of lightning close by, Sarah and Papa stood in the barn doorway, wet to the skin. Papa carried Sarah's chickens. Sarah came with an armful of summer roses.

Sarah's chickens were not afraid, and they settled like small red bundles in the hay. Papa closed the door at last, shutting out some of the sounds of the storm. The barn was eerie and half lighted, like dusk without a lantern. Papa spread blankets around our shoulders and Sarah unpacked a bag of cheese and bread and jam. At the very bottom of the bag were Sarah's shells.

Caleb got up and went over to the small barn window.

"What color is the sea when it storms?" he asked Sarah.

"Blue," said Sarah, brushing her wet hair back with her fingers. "And gray and green."

Caleb nodded and smiled.

"Look," he said to her. "Look what is missing from your drawing."

Sarah went to stand between Caleb and Papa by the window. She looked a long time without speaking. Finally, she touched Papa's shoulder.

"We have squalls in Maine, too," she said. "Just like this. It will be all right, Jacob."

Papa said nothing. But he put his arm around her, and leaned over to rest his chin in her hair. I closed my eyes, suddenly remembering Mama and Papa standing that way, Mama smaller than Sarah, her hair fair against Papa's shoulder. When I opened my eyes again, it was Sarah standing there. Caleb looked at me and smiled and smiled until he could smile no more.

We slept in the hay all night, waking when the wind was wild, sleeping again when it was quiet. And at dawn there was the sudden sound of hail, like stones tossed against the barn. We stared out the window, watching the ice marbles bounce on the ground. And when it was over we opened the barn door and walked out into the early-morning light. The hail crunched and melted beneath our feet. It was white and gleaming for as far as we looked, like sun on glass. Like the sea.

9

It was very quiet. The dogs leaned down to eat the hailstones. Seal stepped around them and leaped up on the fence to groom herself. A tree had blown over near the cow pond. And the wild roses were scattered on the ground, as if a wedding had come and gone there. "I'm glad I saved an armful" was all that Sarah said.

Only one field was badly damaged, and Sarah and Papa hitched up the horses and plowed and replanted during the next two days. The roof had held.

"I told you I know about roofs," Sarah told Papa, making him smile.

Papa kept his promise to Sarah. When the work was done, he took her out into the fields,

Papa riding Jack who was sly, and Sarah riding Old Bess. Sarah was quick to learn.

"Too quick," Caleb complained to me as we watched from the fence. He thought a moment. "Maybe she'll fall off and have to stay here. Why?" he asked, turning to me. "Why does she have to go away alone?"

"Hush up, Caleb," I said crossly. "Hush up."

"I could get sick and make her stay here," said Caleb.

"No."

"We could tie her up."

"No."

And Caleb began to cry, and I took him inside the barn where we could both cry.

Papa and Sarah came to hitch the horses to the wagon, so Sarah could practice driving. Papa didn't see Caleb's tears, and he sent him with an ax to begin chopping up the tree by the pond for firewood. I stood and watched Sarah, the reins in her hands, Papa next to her in the wagon. I could see Caleb standing by the pond, one hand shading his eyes, watching, too. I went into the safe darkness of the barn then, Sarah's chickens scuttling along behind me.

"Why?" I asked out loud, echoing Caleb's question.

The chickens watched me, their eyes small and bright.

The next morning Sarah got up early and put on her blue dress. She took apples to the barn. She loaded a bundle of hay on the wagon for Old Bess and Jack. She put on her yellow bonnet.

"Remember Jack," said Papa. "A strong hand."

"Yes, Jacob."

"Best to be home before dark," said Papa. "Driving a wagon is hard if there's no full moon."

"Yes, Jacob."

Sarah kissed us all, even my father, who looked surprised.

"Take care of Seal," she said to Caleb and me. And with a whisper to Old Bess and a stern word to Jack, Sarah climbed up in the wagon and drove away.

"Very good," murmured Papa as he watched. And after a while he turned and went out into the fields.

Caleb and I watched Sarah from the porch. Caleb took my hand, and the dogs lay down beside us. It was sunny, and I remembered another time when a wagon had taken Mama away. It had been a day just like this day. And Mama had never come back.

Seal jumped up to the porch, her feet making a small thump. Caleb leaned down and picked her up and walked inside. I took the broom and slowly swept the porch. Then I watered Sarah's plants. Caleb cleaned out the wood stove and carried the ashes to the barn, spilling them so that I had to sweep the porch again.

"I *am* loud and pesky," Caleb cried suddenly. "You said so! And she has gone to buy a train ticket to go away!"

"No, Caleb. She would tell us."

"The house is too small," said Caleb. "That's what it is."

"The house is not too small," I said.

I looked at Sarah's drawing of the fields pinned up on the wall next to the window.

"What is missing?" I asked Caleb. "You said you knew what was missing."

"Colors," said Caleb wearily. "The colors of the sea."

Outside, clouds moved into the sky and went away again. We took lunch to Papa, cheese and bread and lemonade. Caleb nudged me.

"Ask him. Ask Papa."

"What has Sarah gone to do?" I asked.

"I don't know," said Papa. He squinted at me. Then he sighed and put one hand on Caleb's head, one on mine. "Sarah is Sarah. She does things her way, you know."

"I know," said Caleb very softly.

Papa picked up his shovel and put on his hat.

"Ask if she's coming back," whispered Caleb.

"Of course she's coming back," I said. "Seal is here." But I would not ask the question. I was afraid to hear the answer.

We fed the sheep, and I set the table for dinner. Four plates. The sun dropped low over the west fields. Lottie and Nick stood at the door, wagging their tails, asking for supper. Papa came to light the stove. And then it was dusk. Soon it would be dark. Caleb sat on the porch steps, turning his moon snail shell over and over in his hand. Seal brushed back and forth against him.

Suddenly Lottie began to bark, and Nick jumped off the porch and ran down the road.

"Dust!" cried Caleb. He climbed the porch and stood on the roof. "Dust, and a yellow bonnet!"

Slowly the wagon came around the windmill and the barn and the windbreak and into the yard, the dogs jumping happily beside it.

"Hush, dogs," said Sarah. And Nick leaped up into the wagon to sit by Sarah.

Papa took the reins and Sarah climbed down from the wagon.

Caleb burst into tears.

"Seal was very worried!" he cried.

Sarah put her arms around him, and he wailed into her dress. "And the house is too small, we thought! And I am loud and pesky!"

Sarah looked at Papa and me over Caleb's head.

"We thought you might be thinking of leaving us," I told her. "Because you miss the sea."

Sarah smiled.

"No," she said. "I will always miss my old home, but the truth of it is I would miss you more."

Papa smiled at Sarah, then he bent quickly to unhitch the horses from the wagon. He led them to the barn for water.

Sarah handed me a package.

"For Anna," she said. "And Caleb. For all of us."

The package was small, wrapped in brown paper with a rubber band around it. Very carefully I unwrapped it, Caleb peering closely. Inside were three colored pencils.

"Blue," said Caleb slowly, "and gray. And green."

Sarah nodded.

Suddenly Caleb grinned.

"Papa," he called. "Papa, come quickly! Sarah has brought the sea!"

We eat our night meal by candlelight, the four of us. Sarah has brought candles from town. And nasturtium seeds for her garden, and a book of songs to teach us. It is late, and Caleb is nearly sleeping by his plate and Sarah is smiling at my father. Soon there will be a wedding. Papa says that when the preacher asks if he will have Sarah for his wife, he will answer, "Ayuh."

Autumn will come, then winter, cold with a wind that blows like the wind off the sea in Maine. There will be nests of curls to look for, and dried flowers all winter long. When there are storms, Papa will stretch a rope from the door to the barn so we will not be lost when we feed the sheep and the cows and Jack and Old Bess. And Sarah's chickens, if they aren't living in the house. There will be Sarah's sea, blue and gray and green, hanging on the wall. And songs, old ones and new. And Seal with yellow eyes. And there will be Sarah, plain and tall.

Skylark

Skylark

Patricia MacLachlan

This is for Emily MacLachlan—
with admiration
with love

Papa married Sarah on a summer day. There were no clouds in the sky, and Papa picked Sarah up in his arms and whirled her around and around, her white dress and veil surrounding them like the summer wind. Caleb was so excited and happy, he burst into tears.

Everybody was happy.

1

"Stand on that stump, Caleb. Anna, you next to him. That will be a good family picture."

Joshua, the photographer, looked through his big camera at us as we stood on the porch squinting in the sunlight. Caleb wore a white shirt, his hair combed slick to his head, Sarah in a white dress, Papa looking hot and uneasy in his suit. The lace at my neck itched in the summer heat. We had to be still for so long that Caleb began to whistle softly, making Sarah smile.

Far off in the distance the dogs, Nick and Lottie, walked slowly through the dry prairie grass. They walked past the cow pond nearly empty of water, past the wagon, past the chickens in the yard. Nick saw us first, then

Lottie, and they began to run. Caleb looked sideways at me as they jumped the fence and ran to us, running up to stand between Sarah and Papa as if they wanted to be in the picture, too. We tried not to laugh, but Sarah couldn't help it. She looked up at Papa and he smiled down at her. And Joshua took the picture of us all laughing, Papa smiling at Sarah.

Joshua laughed, too.

"Your aunts will like that picture," he said to Sarah.

Sarah fanned herself.

"They hardly know what I look like anymore," she said softly. "I hardly know what *they* look like anymore."

I looked at Caleb. I knew Caleb didn't like to think about Sarah and her aunts and her brother and the sea she had left behind.

"It's Maine you came from, isn't it?" said Joshua.

"Yes," said Sarah.

"She lives *here* now," said Caleb loudly.

Papa put his hand on Caleb's head.

"That she does," said Joshua, smiling.

He turned and looked out over the cornfield, the plants so dry they rattled in the wind.

"But I bet Maine is green," Joshua said in a low voice. He looked out over the land with a faraway look, as if he were somewhere else. "We sure could use rain. I remember a long time ago, you remember it, Jacob. The water dried up, the fields so dry that the leaves fell like dust. And then the winds came. My grandfather packed up his family and left."

"Did he come back?" asked Caleb.

Joshua turned.

"No," he said, "he never came back."

Joshua packed up the last of his things and got up in his wagon.

Papa looked at Sarah.

"It will rain," he said.

We watched the wagon go off down the road.

"It will rain," Papa repeated softly.

"Will you worry if it doesn't rain?" asked Caleb.

"Yes, but we'll get along," said Papa. "We always get along."

"Imagine having to *leave*," said Sarah.

Papa took off his jacket.

"We'd never leave, Sarah," he said. "We were born here. Our names are written in this land."

When Papa and Sarah went inside, Caleb looked at me. I knew what he was going to say, and I didn't want to hear it.

"Sarah wasn't born here," he said.

I picked up the pail of grain for the chickens.

"I know that, Caleb," I said crossly. "Papa knows it, too."

Caleb took a stick and bent down in the dirt. I watched him write SARA. He looked up at me.

"I'm writing Sarah's name in the land," he said.

"You can't even spell, Caleb," I said. "You can't."

I walked away. When I turned to look at Caleb, he was staring at me. I wanted to say I was sorry for being cross with him. But I didn't.

"Happily ever after," said Caleb when Papa married Sarah. "Now we'll live happily ever after. That's what the stories say."

Caleb said that all through the summer and the fall when the prairie grasses turned yellow, and through the first winter Sarah and Papa were married. He said it all winter long, when the wind blew around the corners of the house and ice sat slick on the windows. He said it when he fell through the ice on the slough and had to sit in a tub of warm water, his teeth chattering.

"I like the sound of it," Caleb told me. "Happily ever after."

2

The days grew hotter, the sun beating down on us. We stayed inside as much as we could. Even Nick and Lottie stayed inside, stretched out on the wood floor to keep cool. Papa walked the fields, measuring the level of the water in the well over and over, waiting for rain. He came in bringing the dirt with him.

"Papa!" I poked at his feet with my broom. "Your boots!"

I was sweeping, trying to keep the dust out. Sarah was scrubbing the kitchen floor on her hands and knees.

Papa was hot and tired.

"That may be the last washing for the floor," he said to Sarah. "We have to save water."

"That's a mixed blessing," Sarah said, brushing the hair off her face. She watched Caleb feed Seal.

"Don't feed her too much, Caleb," said Sarah. "She's getting fat with your food."

Papa looked closely at Seal. "I think she's more than fat, Sarah."

Sarah looked up. "What?"

"What does he mean?" asked Caleb.

I smiled.

"Kittens. He means kittens, Caleb," I said.

Caleb and I spoke at the same time.

"Can we keep them all?" I asked.

"When will she have them, Papa?" asked Caleb, excited.

"Don't know, Caleb," said Papa, drinking water from the tin cup.

Sarah sat back.

"Has she ever had kittens before, Sarah?" asked Papa.

Sarah shook her head.

"No, never."

Papa smiled at Sarah's look. She stared at Seal for a long time.

"Kittens," she said, her face suddenly breaking into a smile. "Kittens!"

Late light fell across the bedroom, the windows closed to the prairie wind.

I held Sarah's wedding dress up to me and looked in the mirror.

"Anna?"

I jumped, startled, and Sarah smiled at me.

"I didn't mean to frighten you," she said.

I looked in the mirror again.

"Someday I'll marry and move to my husband's land. That's what Papa says."

"Oh he does, does he?" said Sarah.

"That's what you did, Sarah. You came from Maine to marry Papa," I told her.

Sarah was silent for a moment. She sat on the bed.

"Yes," she said slowly. "I guess I did."

"You fell in love with us," said Caleb in the doorway.

"I did that," she said. "First your letters. Then you."

"Did you fall in love with Papa's letters, too? Before you knew him?" asked Caleb.

I sat on the bed and watched Sarah's face as she remembered.

"Yes, I loved your Papa's letters," said Sarah softly. "I loved what was between the lines most."

"What was between the lines?" Caleb asked.

Sarah looked at me when she answered.

"His life," she said simply. "That was what was between the lines."

"Papa's not always good with words," I said.

"Sometimes, yes," said Sarah, laughing. "But when I read your Papa's letters, I could see this farm, and the animals and the sky. And you. Sometimes, what people choose to write down on paper is more important than what they say."

Caleb didn't know what Sarah meant. But I knew. I wrote in my journal every night. And when I read what I had written, I could see myself there, clearer than when I looked in the mirror. I could see all of us: Papa, who couldn't always say the things he felt; Caleb, who said everything; and Sarah, who didn't know that she had changed us all.

Sarah loved the snow.

"We don't have drifts of snow in Maine," she said.

She waited and watched for it so she could paint the prairie snow with morning sun on it. She taught me to paint with watercolors, too. We painted the barn and tree by the cow pond, and we painted the sky just after sunset, Sarah's favorite time.

"When you can't tell where the color comes from," Sarah said.

3

On Sunday the air was still, the way it is before a storm. We dressed up and rode the wagon to church. Inside the church it was cool, like a prairie spring, and Caleb fell asleep. Matthew, Maggie, Rose, and Violet, our closest neighbors, sat in front of us. Tom, their baby, turned around and reached out to Sarah. She smiled and took his hand. Papa smiled, too. We all hated to go outside into the sun again.

Maggie and Sarah walked to the wagons, shading their eyes against the sun.

"Any news?" asked Maggie.

"Seal is having babies," said Caleb. "Lots of babies!"

Maggie laughed.

"That's big news. Come to think of it, I've seen Seal at our house," said Maggie. "With Sam. The orange cat."

Sarah smiled.

"So it's Sam, is it?"

Sarah and Maggie laughed together. Then Sarah reached over and took Tom in her arms. She kissed the top of his head.

"I am surrounded by motherhood," she said softly.

I looked up at the way her voice sounded, sad and thoughtful. "A calf due soon," she added. "Then kittens."

Papa and Matthew came over, Papa's face serious.

"What is it?" asked Sarah. "What's the matter?"

"The church well is down. A whole foot," said Matthew.

"A foot!" exclaimed Maggie. "That's even more than ours."

Papa looked up at the sky.

"What if it doesn't rain?" asked Caleb.

I brushed his arm with my hand as if I were trying to brush away his words.

"It will rain, Caleb," I said.

Tom held out his arms to Papa, and Papa lifted him up, smiling.

"Are those clouds, Tom?" he said. "In the west? Maybe it will rain. Maybe."

"Yes," said Maggie, trying to be cheerful. "It will rain." Her face looked serious suddenly. "It *will* rain," she repeated. "It's just the time before it rains that is hard. It always is."

We rode home followed by clouds of dust tossed up by our wagon. The sky was blue. Heat waves rose off the land. As much as Papa wished for it, there were no clouds in the sky.

"Anna. Anna!"

I opened my eyes and morning sun poured across my quilt. Caleb was there, half dressed.

"What?"

"The calf is born. Hurry!"

Caleb pulled back my covers and I jumped up. We ran downstairs.

"Why didn't you wake us up?" I asked, excited. "When was he born?"

"She," said Papa. He sat at the kitchen table, drinking coffee. "Eat your breakfast first."

Papa drank coffee and Sarah put bowls on the table. Caleb tried to run out the door, but Papa reached out and grabbed him.

"Eat," said Papa firmly.

"Hurry, Caleb! Eat faster," I said.

"I'm eating as fast as I can," said Caleb. "Is Mame excited? Does she like her baby?" he asked Papa.

Papa grinned at Sarah.

"An excited cow? I'm not sure I noticed. What do you think, Sarah?"

"I think she likes her calf," said Sarah, smiling back at Papa.

"What does she look like?" I asked.

"Small, brown," said Papa. "She has some white on her face."

Sarah looked at me over her cup.

"Your Papa says her face is as pale as the winter moon," she said. "And to think that you said that sometimes he is not good with words."

I smiled at Sarah.

"Moonbeam," said Caleb. "We could call her Moonbeam."

Papa laughed at the name.

"Finished," Caleb said, his spoon clattering in the empty bowl.

"Finished," I said.

And we ran out the door to the barn, where in the shadows Mame looked up at us, her eyes steady. After a moment Mame leaned over to lick the calf that lay in the hay.

"Sarah's right," whispered Caleb. "Mame likes her calf."

Papa was right, too. Her face was as pale as the winter moon.

Sometimes Sarah dances, and she makes Papa dance, too, his face shy, his smile like Caleb's smile.

Sometimes, when Papa worries about the farm or the weather, Sarah takes his hand and pulls him outside.

"Come, Jacob, come walk with me," she says.

And he does.

They walk the fields and the country road, Lottie and Nick following them. Once they chased each other through the rows of corn and we could hear the sounds of their laughter.

4

Papa came back from town with letters from Maine. Letters for all of us from Sarah's aunts: Harriet and Mattie and Lou. It was evening, the oil lamp bright in the kitchen. Papa mended a bridle, Caleb leaning against him. I read a letter out loud.

"'There was a storm,' Aunt Mattie says, 'and the porch shingles went to sea. . . .'"

"What does that mean, went to sea?" asked Caleb, interrupting me.

"It means that they blew into the sea," said Sarah with a smile.

I began to read again. "'My hat went to sea, too. The one with the bird on it.'"

Caleb climbed up into Papa's lap.

"A real bird?" exclaimed Caleb.

"Stuffed, Caleb," said Sarah. "Aunt Mattie will miss that hat."

"'Two inches of rain by the glass measure . . .'"

I stopped reading, staring at the word rain. I looked up at Sarah, and she was watching Papa, her face touched by the light from the lamp.

"A glass?" asked Caleb.

I tried to make Caleb stop talking. I didn't want Papa to think about rain.

"What about your letter, Sarah?" said Papa.

Sarah shrugged.

"Just the weather," she said. "Painting William's boat."

Papa looked up at her.

"Read it, Sarah," he said softly.

Sarah took the letter out of her pocket. Slowly she opened it.

"'The grass is green,'" she read. "'Growing so tall that we've cut it dozens of times already. The trees are lush. Autumn will be beautiful. Come visit, all of you. Soon. Love, Mattie.'"

There was a silence in the room. Then

Papa kissed Caleb and got up. He stood at the door, looking out at the red of the setting sun.

"It will be a beautiful sunset tonight," he said, his voice low. "I can tell."

Papa opened the door and went outside.

"A glass to measure rain?" asked Caleb again, still thinking of Mattie's letter.

"Hush, Caleb," I said.

Sarah didn't answer Caleb. She put her letter on the table, walked to the door, and went outside. I picked up the letter. There was more that Sarah hadn't read.

It has rained nearly every afternoon, Mattie had written. *It cools down the day and leaves us with good nights for sleeping.*

I watched Sarah put her hand on Papa's arm as he stood looking over the dry fields.

My eyes filled with tears.

I knew Sarah was sorry about the letters from Maine and the talk of rain.

It's not your fault that Maine is green, Sarah, I thought. *It isn't.*

It was dark and the moon was up when Caleb came in from outside, Nick with him. Sarah looked up from her book.

"Caleb! I thought you'd gone to bed long ago," she said.

"I had something to do," he said. "For Papa."

Sarah smiled and put her arm around him.

"Well, off to bed now. It's late. Both of you."

Caleb yawned and went up the stairs. Sarah went out to the porch. Papa came across the yard from the barn, and he stopped suddenly, then looked at Sarah.

On the fence post between them was a small glass, sitting empty in the moonlight, waiting for rain.

Roses grew on the fence when Sarah came. And the fields were filled with wildflowers. I learned to float in the cow pond and Caleb ran with the sheep in the green fields.

Now clouds come and go, and the hot winds, too. But there is no rain for the roses. Dirt from the fields blows over everything, and the leaves have crumbled. "Like dust," Joshua said when he took our picture.

Like dust.

5

Each day Papa dropped a rope with a stone down the well to measure the water level.

"Is it past the mark?" asked Sarah.

Papa nodded.

"How much, Jacob?"

Papa held out his hands a foot apart.

Caleb and I got up into the wagon to go to town.

"Soon we'll have to haul water for the animals," said Papa.

"We can do that," said Sarah.

"We'll have to measure out our own water," said Papa as he climbed up.

"But we already do that, Jacob."

Papa looked down at Sarah.

"We'll have to use less."

Sarah stared at Papa, then got up to sit next to him.

"We can do that, too," she said firmly.

We drove off down the road. After a while Caleb poked his head between Sarah and Papa. Papa looked at him.

"So, Caleb?"

"*I* put the glass on the post," said Caleb.

Papa nodded but didn't say anything.

"To measure the rain when it comes," Caleb added.

"Thank you for that," said Papa.

"You're welcome," said Caleb happily.

He sat back in the wagon and folded his arms. Papa smiled.

All the way to town I looked for green. But as far as I could see the fields were brown. The wheat fields were dry. Turkey vultures circled in the distance. There was no green.

Everything seemed slow in town, as if the

heat had taken over. Papa left the wagon in the shade of the granary and slowly unloaded his last bags of grain from the wagon. Slowly he walked inside.

Mrs. Parkley's store was cool. Rose and Violet were there, Rose carrying Tom, who smiled at me. But Maggie had her arms around Caroline, who was crying.

"Caroline? What's wrong, Maggie?" said Sarah.

"Their well is dry," Maggie said softly.

"Caroline," said Sarah. "What can we do?"

"There's nothing to do," Caroline said, drying her tears. "We've already packed up."

"Packed up!" said Sarah, shocked. "Where will you go?"

"They have family," said Maggie.

Caroline took her packages and went to the door. She turned suddenly, her face sad.

"Joseph says we'll come back," she said. "But we won't. I know we won't."

She opened the door and left. Maggie walked over to the door and looked out.

"Surely we can do something," Sarah said. "We could haul water, Maggie. We would all work harder."

Sarah's voice grew louder, and Caleb moved closer to me.

"You can't just give up!" said Sarah. "You can't just give up everything you've worked for. . . ."

Maggie whirled around, her face angry.

"You don't know how hard this is, Sarah," she said, angrily. "You haven't been in this kind of trouble before!"

Sarah stared at Maggie, then at the others in the store. Maggie reached over and took Sarah's hand. She opened the door and pulled her outside. I watched the two of them cross the dusty street. Maggie's arm went around Sarah, but they kept walking. Papa came out from the granary and watched them, too, Matthew beside him.

"Is Sarah angry?" asked Caleb.

I looked down at his worried face.

"No," I said. "Sarah's not angry."

Caleb sighed.

"Sarah likes to make things right," he said.

We watched without speaking, and then Joseph and Caroline's wagon passed, all packed with chairs and clothes and a cupboard, pots and pans tied on. Sarah turned to watch it, and Papa watched, too, from across the street. And then the wagon turned a corner and was gone.

6

The ride home from town was quiet, the wind blowing dust around us.

"Any news in town?" asked Sarah wearily.

"Some news," said Papa. "Good news."

"Good news? What good news?"

"Your birthday is coming soon. Mattie wrote to remind me."

"She didn't!"

"She did," said Papa. "So—what do you want? Jewels, silk, travel?"

Sarah laughed.

"Travel? Where would I go, Jacob?"

"Somewhere green," said Papa. "Somewhere cool."

Sarah looked at Papa.

"Do you think I would *leave*?" asked Sarah softly.

Papa was silent.

"Can we sing, Sarah?" asked Caleb.

"It's too hot, Caleb," she said. "Too hot for singing."

Papa flicked the reins over the horses' backs, but they wouldn't go faster.

"It's even too hot for Jack and Old Bess," he said.

I leaned back against the empty grain sacks and took out my journal, but it lay in my lap.

Caleb moved over close to me.

"Why aren't you writing?"

"There's nothing new to write," I said, lifting my hair off my neck. "There's nothing good. Just the heat. The fields are dried up. There's no rain."

"There will be rain," said Caleb. "Papa said so." He pointed. "That was the field where the wildflowers grew, remember, when Sarah came? The pond was full then. We went swimming and fell asleep in the grass."

I stared at Caleb, then out at the fields, remembering when the fields were green. Remembering when the days were cool. Remembering when Sarah came by train and Caleb and I were afraid that she'd miss the sea.

Suddenly, Caleb stood up.

"Papa! Fire!"

In the west meadow a thread of smoke rose.

"Hold on," yelled Papa.

Sarah dropped to the wagon floor, and we held on as the horses raced for the yard.

Papa jumped down.

"Soak the grain sacks in the pond water! Hurry!"

Sarah and Papa ran to beat out the flames. We could see red flames in the dry grasses now. Caleb and I soaked the sacks, then ran closer to the fire, water dripping down our clothes.

"Stay back," warned Papa. "There's a wind coming up."

Nick and Lottie ran from the barn, barking.

And then suddenly Sarah screamed. Her skirt was on fire. Papa turned and threw Sarah to the ground and smothered the flames with a sack. He pulled her up.

"Are you all right?"

When Sarah nodded, Papa began to shout at her.

"I told you to stay back. You never listen! I *told* you there was wind!"

Caleb took my hand.

Sarah began beating the fire, now nearly out.

"You can't put out the fire alone!" she shouted. "Stop yelling at me!"

And then there was only smoke, the grasses all black and smoldering. Papa beat at one small flame. He stood back, and there was silence. Nick and Lottie stopped barking.

"We'll have to watch for fires all the time, now, even at night," said Papa, out of breath.

Sarah and Papa began walking back to the house. Sarah's hair was down; her clothes were wet and sooty. Papa looked at her, then away.

"You're a sight, you know," he said softly.

Sarah didn't answer.

Papa looked at her again, then smiled a small smile.

"You look . . . beautiful," he said.

I held my breath. I had never heard Papa say such a thing to Sarah.

Sarah kept on walking. Then she turned and looked at him.

"Do you *really* think I would leave?" she said. "Just for somewhere cool? Somewhere *green?*"

This time Papa was silent. The two of them walked away from the blackened grass, past the dogs, and past us just as if we weren't there.

And that night, when Papa went out to close the barn door, Sarah ran after him. I saw them from my window. Papa took Sarah in his arms and kissed her, and they turned around and around and around, dust swirling over them in a cloud.

My dreams are cool. They are cool and the color of the sky before rain, a dark and peaceful blue, the clouds edged in black before the rain comes and the earth smells sharp and sweet. I remember that smell.

The days are hot and still now.

Only my dreams are cool.

7

We sat on the porch out of the terrible sun, Maggie fanning herself, Sarah mixing batter for biscuits. Rose and Violet rolled a ball in the dirt to Tom. Caleb sat watching the sky for clouds.

"This heat," said Maggie wearily. "I dream of my old home sometimes. And I dream of long, cool mornings of sleep without the baby waking!"

Sarah smiled.

"Night dreams or daydreams?" she asked.

"What's a day dream?" asked Caleb.

Sarah sat back and looked at Tom crawling happily in the dirt.

"Sometimes, no matter where you are, you think of something sweet and cool. A place, maybe. And suddenly it's there. Or maybe it's something you wish for . . . and it is so near you can touch it, smell it . . . hear the sound of it . . ."

Sarah looked up suddenly as if caught up in her thoughts.

"She's dreaming about Maine," Caleb whispered to me.

No. It's not Maine, I thought. *It's not Maine she's thinking about. It's something else.*

Tom grabbed the ball and held it over his head. Sarah smiled.

"I have dreams, Sarah," Caleb said.

"Good dreams, Caleb?" she asked.

"I dream about rain," said Caleb. "Do you? Do you dream about rain?"

Sarah reached over and took Caleb on her lap.

"Yes, Caleb. I dream about rain."

"Good," he said. "Then it will come true."

But rain was only in our dreams. The winds came every day, blowing dust through the windows and into the house until it covered the furniture and got into the food and our clothes and hair. The land got even drier, and we stopped taking baths. Every day we hauled river water for the animals in big wooden barrels.

And then the worst thing happened.

We drove to the river in our wagon, empty barrels in the back. Clouds hung high in the sky. Maggie sat in her wagon by the riverbed. Matthew stood on the bluff over the river, looking down.

"Hello, Maggie," called Sarah.

But Maggie didn't speak. She didn't even look at us.

We got down from the wagon. The river was nearly dry, only a small trickle in the red prairie dirt.

Everyone was quiet.

"What will we do?" whispered Sarah.

"We'll have to travel farther for water," said Papa.

"Think about it, Jacob," said Matthew. "It will be a three-day trip, maybe four. When we get back home, then what? Water for the crops? There *are* no crops."

Papa looked at Matthew, then away over the land.

Matthew sighed.

"Maggie and I have been talking about another way," he said.

"What?" asked Sarah.

"I think that what Matthew means is that they're thinking about leaving," said Papa softly.

Sarah turned and looked up at Maggie in the wagon.

"Leaving?" she said, her voice rough and dry like the fields.

Maggie climbed down and went behind the wagon, Sarah following her. I walked closer and stood out of sight, and saw Sarah put out her hand to touch Maggie. But Maggie took a step away, as if Sarah's comfort was too hard. And I heard words I wish I hadn't heard.

"I hate this land," said Sarah. "I don't have to love it the way Matthew and Jacob love it.

They give it everything. Everything! And it gives nothing back."

"They don't know anywhere else, Sarah," said Maggie.

I closed my eyes, but I couldn't close out Sarah's words.

"Jacob once said his name was written in this land, but mine isn't. It isn't!" said Sarah angrily.

"You are like the prairie lark, you know," said Maggie. "It sings its song above the land to let all the birds know it's there before it plunges down to earth to make its home. But you have not come to earth, Sarah."

There was silence then, and I opened my eyes again.

"You don't have to love this land," said Maggie. "But if you don't love it, you won't survive. Jacob's right. You have to write your name in the land to live here."

Sarah didn't speak. She took a handful of dry prairie grass in her hands, letting it crumble through her fingers. Then she walked away from us, through the dried grass, out onto the brown prairie that stretched all the way to the sky. She stood there all alone until Papa went to tell her it was time to go home.

We hung wildflowers from the ceiling to dry them for winter, I remember. Sarah cut our hair, tossing it into the fields so the birds could use it for nests.

And we sang.

When Sarah read books with us, even her words were like a song.

8

Sarah and I sat in the kitchen. The air was thick with the heat, and there was no breeze. There hadn't been any wind for days. Sarah was writing a letter to the aunts in Maine. I wrote in my journal.

"Remember the wildflowers?" I asked Sarah. "And the roses that grew on the fence? Remember singing?"

Sarah looked up.

"Yes," she said. She reached out and touched my hair. "I remember."

"Papa! Papa! Coyote!" shouted Caleb from outside.

Sarah and I ran outside. By the paddock fence a thin coyote was drinking water out of the water pail.

"He'll kill Moonbeam!" shouted Caleb.

Papa came from the field, took a step toward the coyote, then turned and ran to the house. He came out with his rifle.

"Jacob! What are you going to do?" cried Sarah.

"Go inside, Sarah," he said.

Papa raised his rifle to shoot the coyote, but Sarah grabbed the barrel of the rifle.

"No! Don't do it, Jacob. Don't!"

"Sarah! Stop!" yelled Papa.

Papa tried to push her away, and the coyote looked up at the sound of their voices. Slowly he ran away over the fields, stopping once to look back. Then he was gone.

Sarah began to cry.

"He only wanted water. Water, Jacob!"

Caleb climbed over the paddock fence and stood next to me. Papa took Sarah's arm and turned to Caleb.

"Put the animals in the barn, Caleb," he said.

Caleb turned and walked to the barn.

Tears streamed down Sarah's face.

"Water!" she said. "He only wanted water. Just like us. . . ."

She slumped to the ground and put her hands over her face as she cried.

"Get Sarah something to drink, Anna," said Papa.

He took off his hat and sat down on the ground next to her.

"Anna," he said sharply. "Now!"

I turned and went to the water barrel and scooped out a cup of water. Papa put his arms around Sarah.

His voice was soft.

"Sarah. Sarah," he said softly. "It will be all right. It will be all right."

But Sarah cried and cried. And when Papa turned and looked at me, I knew that nothing was all right.

The look in his eyes was fear.

And that night, when I came in from the barn to go to bed, there was something else missing from the fence. Missing like Sarah's roses. Caleb's glass was gone.

"They're coming!" said Caleb, looking out the upstairs window.

He wore a clean shirt, and his hair was brushed smooth. I wore the dress I had worn when Papa and Sarah were married. Outside, wagons came into the yard.

"Will this make Sarah happy?" Caleb asked me, worried.

I watched more wagons drive in. I saw Maggie dressed in a rose dress and a straw hat.

"Yes," I said. "This will make Sarah happy."

"Anna? Caleb? What is this?" said Sarah in the bedroom doorway.

We whirled around, silent. Sarah walked to the window to look out, too, but I took her hand and pulled her out into the hallway. Papa looked up the stairs at her. He wore a vest and his hair was slicked back. He smiled at her.

"Happy birthday, Sarah," he said.

"There are guests. And presents, Sarah!" said Caleb.

"But I'm not dressed," said Sarah.

"Then get dressed," said Papa softly.

Outside there was a table in the shade of the house, set with food and lemonade. Maggie and Matthew were there, and Rose and Violet and the baby. All the neighbors were there, too. Papa carried something covered with a cloth out to the table.

"What is it?" asked Maggie.

"You'll see," said Papa.

"Here she is!" someone said.

We all turned, and Sarah came out on the porch in her white dress.

"Happy birthday, Sarah," said Papa.

"Happy birthday," everyone called.

Sarah smiled at the sight of them, everyone washed and clean as if the prairie winds had stopped covering us all with dust.

"A present from the aunts," said Papa.

He took the cloth away, and there was a phonograph. I handed him a record and he put the needle on it. Suddenly, music filled the yard. Sarah stared. Papa walked up to her and held out his hand. She smiled and came down the steps and they began to dance. Maggie and Matthew began to dance, too, the baby between them. Everyone danced, then, in the dirt yard, the light around them all yellow like an old photograph. Sarah buried her face in Papa's shoulder, and Caleb smiled at me. And for a little while, as the sun began to set, as they danced, everyone forgot about the drought. For a while, everyone was happy again. Even Sarah. Even Papa.

The last of the wagons left in the moonlight. Sarah and Papa waved good-bye. Caleb was asleep under the table and Papa took him off to bed. Then Papa helped Sarah carry the phonograph inside.

"I have a present for you, Sarah," I said. I handed her a small book.

"Anna, what is this?" said Sarah.

"It's a book I started. About you. About our family," I said.

Papa went out to the porch. Sarah sat down and opened the book. She began to read.

"'When my mother . . .'"

She stopped and looked at me. Then she began to read again. Papa stood outside the screen door, listening.

"'When my mother, Sarah, came, she came by train. I didn't know I'd love her, but Caleb did. Papa didn't know, either, but he does love her. I have seen them kiss.'" Sarah smiled at me. "'And I have seen the way he looks at her and the way he touches her hair. My mother, Sarah, doesn't love the prairie. She tries, but she can't help remembering what she knew first.'"

Sarah stopped and closed the book, holding it close to her.

"You like it," I said.

"I like it," said Sarah softly.

She put her arms around me, and I saw Papa watching us.

Sarah got up, then, and went to the door.

"It was a fine party, Jacob."

She put her hand up and he did, too, so that they touched through the screen.

"I'd almost forgotten music," whispered Sarah.

Then she looked past Papa at the fence post.

"Where's Caleb's glass, Jacob?"

Papa didn't speak.

"Put it back, please, Jacob," said Sarah. "It should be there when it rains."

Papa stared at Sarah. And when I went to bed later that night, I looked out and saw it there, shining and clean, on the fence post.

9

The next day, after the party, after the music and dancing, Matthew and Maggie's well went dry. They drove their wagon to our house to say good-bye, and I could hardly look at Sarah's face.

The wagon was packed with furniture and clothes; Rose and Violet sat in the back, the baby on Maggie's lap.

"I'm sorry to be leaving you, Jacob," said Matthew.

"It's all right, Matthew. I know," said Papa.

"I'll miss you," Sarah said to Maggie. Her face was tight, to keep all her feelings from coming out. She reached out to touch the baby's hand.

"We'll be back," said Maggie.

Tears came down her face.

"We'll be back," she repeated.

The baby began to cry as the wagon drove out of the yard. When Sarah turned to look at Papa, tears sat at the corners of her eyes.

"They'll be back," said Papa.

He watched the cloud of dust that followed Matthew's wagon down the road, his eyes narrowed against the sunlight.

That night I dreamed about roses, and green fields, and water. A glass of water on the fence post, and ponds of water to swim in; Caleb spitting streams of water in the air like a whale. Sarah laughing and splashing us with water.

A sharp clap of thunder woke me. Lottie and Nick barked as lightning lit up the sky. I turned over in bed, but then Papa's voice from downstairs made me sit up.

"Sarah! Sarah! It's fire!"

I got up and rushed to the window, and there was fire in the field close to the barn. Flames creeping up the fence, flames near the corral.

I ran downstairs and out to the porch, Caleb behind me. Sarah was running carrying wet sacks, her hair down her back. Sarah and Papa beat the flames around the corral. Then Papa stopped to let the frightened horses out.

"Get the cows," he shouted to Sarah.

Sarah ran to the barn and pulled the cows outside.

"Shoo! Shoo!" she cried.

Caleb ran down to get Moonbeam.

"Get on the porch and stay there," Sarah shouted at him as he led Moonbeam away.

I put my arm around Caleb. I could feel him trembling.

Sarah screamed as some hay caught fire and the side of the barn burst into flame.

"Buckets!" shouted Papa. "Get buckets of water! Buckets!"

Sarah ran to the barrel and filled a bucket,

running back to him as the fire grew. Papa grabbed it and then Sarah stopped him. I couldn't hear what she said, but I knew what it was. It was the last barrel. Papa stopped, then, and stared at the barn as flames caught the dry wood and then the roof. Sparks flew everywhere. And then part of the roof fell and Sarah and Papa moved back. Sarah put her arm around Papa as the barn burned. They stood there watching for a long time. Papa turned once to look away from the fire and I could see his eyes, shining red from the fire.

I had never seen Papa's face so sad.

The sun came up in the morning the way it always did. But everything had changed. The barn was gone, only a few blackened timbers standing. The cows walked in the yard, the sheep in the cornfield, looking for green grass. I stood at my window and watched Sarah and Papa talking by the clothesline. I saw her shake her head, no. I saw Papa take her hand. She shook her head again. Then Papa put his arms around her.

I knew we would have to go away.

They told us at dinnertime.

"Maine?" said Caleb. "Are you coming, too, Papa?"

Papa shook his head and looked at Sarah.

"I have to stay here," he said softly. "I can't go away from the land."

"Can Seal and the dogs come?" Caleb asked.

Papa shook his head.

"They'll be happier here," he said. "I'll take care of them."

"What will you do while we're gone, Papa?" asked Caleb.

"I'll miss you," Papa said softly, reaching out to take Caleb's hand. He looked at me, then, and as if he knew I would cry if I spoke, he took my hand, too.

"What will happen to us?" I asked after a moment.

Papa looked at Sarah, and his words were for her.

"We will write letters," he said, his voice soft. "We've written letters before, you know."

10

We traveled three days and nights on the train across the dry prairies. We passed packed wagons. We passed through towns and cities. We slept to the clackety sound of the train and woke with the red sun. Caleb was excited, looking out the window. Sarah was tired and sad. Sometimes I read to her from my journal.

"'When Sarah came, she wore a yellow bonnet,'" I read. "'She brought Seal to us. The corn was high and the wheat all yellow. We lay down with the sheep in the fields, and Sarah taught us how to swim.

"'When they were married, my mother, Sarah, wore a dress soft like mist, and a veil. I think Papa cried. . . .'"

Sarah turned to me. "Did he?" she asked, her voice soft. "Did he cry?"

I smiled and Sarah closed her eyes. I covered her with a shawl.

We went over a bridge, the river shining in the sun.

Caleb turned from the window. "Sarah?"

Sarah opened her eyes.

"Is this the way you came?" he asked.

Sarah looked out at the land. "Yes, Caleb," she said softly. "This is the way I came."

Maine was green. When we got off the train, Sarah stood still. She looked at the train station, and at the trees, and at the people.

"Sarah?" I said.

"It's all right, Anna," said Sarah. "It's just what you wrote in your book. I've come back to what I knew first."

"Sarah! Sarah Wheaton!"

A man waved to Sarah. He wore a vest and a gold chain across it.

Sarah smiled.

"Chub!" she said. "You're still here!"

The man hugged Sarah.

"Where would I be?" he said. "Except dead, maybe. Are the hens meeting you?"

Sarah laughed.

"No. And I'm Sarah Witting now. These are my children, Anna and Caleb. Can you take us there?"

"Get in."

We got in Chub's car, open all around, with shining brass trim and wood on the side.

"I've never been in a car before," whispered Caleb.

"It's about time you were," said Chub. "Want to drive?"

"No," said Caleb, looking alarmed. Then he smiled at Chub. "I won't tell the aunts you call them hens, either."

Chub laughed. He started the car. We passed green grass and green trees and flowers blooming in green gardens as we drove to the house where Sarah had lived.

And then we saw the sea.

"All that water!" said Caleb, running down

the lawn of the aunts' house. Sarah and I looked out over the water: at cliffs that went down to the sea; at birds that flew over us; at boats with white sails like clouds.

"Come on," said Sarah after a moment. She took our hands. "Let's go meet the aunts."

We walked up the lawn to the house. The house was large with shutters on the windows. There were gardens with flowers I had never seen before.

"Will they like us?" asked Caleb.

"They will love you," said Sarah, laughing. "They will fall upon you with kisses."

We walked up the steps of the big porch. Sarah put out her hand to open the door, but it swung open, and a woman in a silk dress stood there, her feet bare. Her eyes widened when she saw us. Her hand went up to her mouth. Sarah smiled.

"Hello, Mattie," she said softly. "We're home."

The aunts laughed and cried and fed us.

"I loved your letters," said Aunt Mattie. "I loved all the pictures you drew." She kissed Sarah and Caleb and she kissed me. Then she kissed Sarah again.

Aunt Harriet, tall with wire glasses, in bare feet, too, tried to feed us all the food in the kitchen.

"I made these cookies, Anna, Caleb," she said. "Are you tired? I made the bread, too. And the soup! Do you want a nap? Do you want a bath?"

"Harriet, let them be!" said Aunt Mattie.

Sarah leaned over close to us.

"See?" she said. "I told you."

And then Aunt Lou, dressed in overalls and high boots, came in the front door with her dog.

"Lou!" said Sarah.

Aunt Lou hugged Sarah. She hugged me.

"Mind that beast," said Aunt Harriet.

"The beast's name is Brutus," said Aunt Lou.

"Lou works with animals," said Aunt Harriet.

"Lou works with a veterinarian," said Aunt Lou. She kissed Caleb twice. "Harriet wants me in silk and pearls."

Brutus jumped up on Caleb's lap.

"Oh, get away!" scolded Aunt Harriet.

"Dogs like me," said Caleb, smiling. "We have two dogs at home."

"This is what we've needed all along, a child!" said Aunt Lou, hugging Caleb. "We must get ourselves one."

"It looks like we have two," said Aunt Mattie softly.

"Sarah," said Aunt Harriet, "will Jacob be coming, too?"

Sarah looked out the window.

"No," she said softly. "Jacob won't be coming."

"Papa's home," I said.

Somehow hearing my own words made it worse. I started to cry. Sarah put her arms around me, and I cried harder.

"Papa had to stay home."

Maine is green and full of voices and people laughing and talking; the tide going in and going out; the moon rising above the water. Sarah loves it here. The last thing every night she walks by the water, and the first thing in the morning she is there, too. Now I know how much she missed her old home. I miss my home. I miss Lottie and Nick and the land and the big sky.

I miss Papa.

11

It took longer for Caleb to miss Papa. Caleb swam every day in the cold water. Aunt Lou wrapped him in blankets when he came out, shivering, his teeth chattering. He went fishing with Aunt Lou and with Sarah's brother, William, who was so happy when he first saw Sarah that he ran up the hill and whirled her around in his arms. It made me think of Papa and Sarah turning around and around in the prairie wind at night.

William's wife, Meg, hugged Sarah, too.

"It's been so long!" she said. "Almost two years since we've seen you!"

Two years. I looked at Sarah and wondered if she was thinking what I was thinking. Would it be two years before we saw Papa?

"William looks like you, Sarah," said Caleb.

"Plain and tall, I told you so," said Sarah. "Remember?"

"Did you hear what I just heard?" said Aunt Harriet as we picnicked on a blanket in the grass by the sea. "Seal is going to have kittens!"

"The father is orange," called Caleb, making the aunts laugh.

"Seal!" exclaimed William. "I remember that Seal was independent. Independent like Sarah."

William put his arm around Sarah. The sun came out from a cloud, but it wasn't hot like home. It was cool and green and beautiful. But it didn't make me happy. I thought about Papa at home by himself, building a barn in the hot sun.

"Where was your dune, Sarah?" asked Caleb.

"Down there," said Sarah, pointing to an inlet.

"I remember when Papa made us a dune," said Caleb softly. He looked up at Sarah. "A dune made of hay. Do you remember?"

"Yes," said Sarah. "I remember, Caleb."

Sarah looked over at me as the aunts talked and laughed. She reached out to touch my arm.

"It's all right, Anna," she said softly. "It's all right."

But it wasn't.

The next week letters came from Papa. Sarah, Caleb, William, and I rowed out in the bay in William's rowboat, and Caleb read his letter.

"'Dear Caleb, Moonbeam is getting bigger every day. I have started building the barn. Still no rain, but yesterday Seal had four kittens!'"

"Four!" said William. Sarah smiled.

"'Three are gray like Seal,'" Caleb read. "'One is orange. Nick and Lottie miss you. Every day they sit looking down the road, waiting for you to come home. I love you.

Give Sarah a kiss from me. Love, Papa.'"

William rowed to shore, and we pulled the boat up.

"Papa misses us, too," I said to Sarah. "When he writes about Nick and Lottie waiting for us. Remember you once said that Papa's letters were full of things between the lines?"

"Yes," said Sarah.

I leaned over and kissed her.

"That's Papa's kiss," I said.

William leaned over to kiss Sarah, too.

"And that's mine," he said.

Dear Anna,

It is quiet here without you. I miss your voices and Sarah's songs. Sometimes, if I close my eyes, I think I can hear them.

Love,

Papa

The aunts played music. Aunt Harriet

played a flute that squeaked sometimes. Aunt Lou played the piano in bare feet, and Brutus watched her pedal. Aunt Mattie danced with a long scarf and a serious look that made Caleb laugh.

Sarah took naps in the afternoons and slept late in the mornings.

Chub drove Sarah away and back again one afternoon. Aunt Lou said she had gone to the doctor.

"Are you sick, Sarah?" I asked her that night.

She smiled at me, a small smile at first, then a big smile.

"No, Anna. I'm not sick."

She was in bed, her long hair down.

"Read me your Papa's letter again," she said.

When I did, she smiled more.

"Sarah?"

We looked up. Caleb stood in the door. He was in his pajamas, his hair all messed from sleep.

"Caleb, what's the matter?" asked Sarah.

"A dream I had," he said softly. "A dream about Papa."

"That's a good dream," said Sarah.

She lifted the covers and Caleb got in bed with her.

"I dreamed that Papa looked and looked and couldn't find us," said Caleb.

"Oh, Caleb," said Sarah, putting her arm around him. "Your Papa knows where we are. He does."

Caleb picked up the family picture that Sarah kept on her bed stand.

"I used to dream about rain, remember?" he said.

Sarah nodded.

"Now I dream about Papa."

There was silence in the room, and then Caleb looked at Sarah.

"Is this our new home, Sarah?" he asked softly.

Sarah didn't answer. She put her arms around him and looked at me over his head. She began to sing very softly.

"Hush little baby, don't say a word.
Papa's gonna buy you a mockingbird.
And if that mockingbird don't sing,
Papa's gonna buy you a diamond ring."

I thought of Joshua, the photographer, who had told us about his grandfather leaving the prairie.

"Did he come back?" Caleb had asked him.

No, he never came back.

And that night I dreamed Caleb's dream: Papa looking for us. He could hear Sarah's song and our voices, and he searched the fields and the house and the barn. But we weren't there.

12

We woke to a new sound. A sound I hadn't heard for months. I ran to the window. Rain.

"Anna!"

I turned, and Caleb and I grinned at each other. We dressed quickly and ran downstairs to the porch. Rain came down, filling the rain gutters. It sent little rivers down the drive-way. Everything smelled sweet. Caleb spread his arms and ran out into the rain in his clothes, racing around the yard. I laughed and ran after him. We jumped and ran, feeling the cool water run down our faces. We looked up, and Sarah stood on the porch. She smiled, and, very slowly, she walked down the steps and lifted her face to the rain. Then she ran down the lawn to take our hands and dance with us.

The aunts came out on the porch to watch.

"Rain!" Sarah called to them. "It's been so long!"

William came up from the water in his yellow slicker and hat to watch, too. Then, laughing, he took off his slicker to dance with us until the aunts made us come up and dry off with towels. We were sorry to see the sun come out.

"I remember you when you were little," William said to Sarah. "Running, climbing. You were always in the trees; out on the rocks. You never stayed still."

Suddenly Sarah looked at William.

"Do you remember a song Papa used to sing about a skylark?" she asked.

William smiled.

"A poem. I only remember the first line: 'Like a skylark Sarah sings!' Papa said you'd never come to earth."

Sarah looked out over the sea, and I knew she was thinking of Maggie's words to her on the dry prairie. Words I wasn't supposed to hear. "You're like the prairie lark, Sarah. You have not come to earth."

That night I wrote Papa a letter.

Dear Papa,

Caleb and I miss you. Sarah misses you, too. We are fine. We went fishing and rowing in William's boat. Sometimes seals poke their heads out of the water to watch us. You would love the sea.

Write soon,

Love, Anna.

P.S. I gave Sarah your kiss.

I didn't tell Papa about the rain.

The aunts had tea in the moonlight. The light lay like a blanket over the water below.

"Have you ever been married, Aunt Harriet?" asked Caleb.

"Caleb! That's private," I said.

But Aunt Harriet smiled. She took Caleb on her lap.

"Private, maybe," she said. "But like everything else, it's history. No, I was never married. Almost, but not quite. I never met a dashing man like your father."

"What's dashing?" asked Caleb.

"That's what I'm doing," said Aunt Lou, coming down the path. She was dressed in a bathrobe. "I'm dashing into the water. Do you want to come? I'm going skinny-dipping."

"Do you mean you're going to swim all naked?!" asked Caleb.

Caleb followed Aunt Lou down the path. And then his voice came up the hill.

"Anna! Come here! In the moonlight she looks like a big fish!"

Aunt Harriet and Aunt Mattie laughed, Aunt Mattie so hard she spilled her tea. And then it was quiet again.

"Everyone goes skinny-dipping," said Sarah. Her voice was soft with memory.

I thought about the pond at home when the

moon came up so big and close it seemed you could touch it. Far off a loon cried on the water. The bell buoy made a lonely, sad sound.

That night, under the same moon that Papa saw, we could see fireworks from the faraway town. Splashes of color in the sky, red and silver and green.

"They're like the dandelions that bloom in the fields at home in summer," I told Sarah.

Sarah reached over and took my hand.

"Do you think the drought's over yet?" asked Caleb, leaning against Sarah.

"No," said Sarah. "It's not over, Caleb. It may be a long time."

Her voice was low, her eyes dark and sad. She looked at me.

A long time. I didn't like those words, *a long time.*

13

More letters came from Papa. The dogs missed us. *Papa missed us.* All our days were long days filled with green all around us, and the sea. The rain should have made us happy, but it didn't. It made us think about Papa. Even Caleb looked sad now. One day Sarah showed him the woolly ragwort that grew in Maine, but it didn't make Caleb laugh the way it used to.

At night Caleb had bad dreams. I could hear him, and I could hear Sarah singing him back to sleep.

Sarah wrote letters to Papa every day. At night she read his letters over and over again, the light from the oil lamp spilling into the hallway.

Dear Anna and Caleb and Sarah,

Somehow it isn't so hot now. The nights are cooler and the dogs are sleeping in my room again. Sometimes Lottie tries to climb up on my bed.

I love you all.

Jacob

And then, one day at dinner, Caleb said something that made my heart skip a beat.

"It's almost time for school," he said.

Fall was almost here, the air cool and crisp in the mornings as if frost would come soon. I had hardly thought about fall and school. My thoughts were about summer, and Papa, and the sweet smell of the prairie grass.

The aunts looked at Sarah, then at Caleb and me.

"Would you like to visit the school here, Caleb?" said Aunt Harriet.

"It's a wonderful school, Caleb," said Sarah slowly. She sighed. "I went to school there."

Caleb stood up and looked at us. Very carefully he pushed in his chair.

"No," he said. "I don't want to go to school here. I like you, but I don't want to live here."

Caleb walked to the door, opened it.

"I want to go home," he said in a soft voice. He looked at Sarah. "Don't you?" he asked. "Don't *you* want to go home, Sarah?" Then he left.

It was quiet. I stared at my plate of food. I could feel Aunt Mattie beside me, fiddling with her fork. Aunt Harriet cleared her throat. When I looked up again, Sarah was staring out the window at the sea. No one spoke.

I looked everywhere for Caleb: behind the house, in the wooden rowboat, on the rocks where the seals sunned. I found him huddled by a driftwood log in the cove. Caleb was crying.

I sat down next to him and listened to the waves come in. A wind came up and I put my arms around him.

"Don't cry, Caleb," I said. "Please don't cry."

After a moment Caleb looked up at me. I could see his eyes shining in the moonlight. I thought of Papa's eyes shining when the barn burned.

"Anna," said Caleb, his voice soft, "will we see Papa again? Ever?"

Caleb waited for me to answer. But I couldn't find any words for him. He began to cry again. And we sat there as clouds moved across the moon—dark, then light, then dark again. Caleb fell asleep.

14

The August sun rose red, then turned gold. It touched the flowers of the aunts' gardens, the beds of late roses and nasturtiums and asters. Geese flew in, sitting calmly on the water. A boat with two masts and a tall sail slipped by. Caleb went fishing with William and came home with two fish.

"Flounder," said William, smiling at us.

But Caleb didn't smile.

In the afternoon we walked by the water, Aunt Lou and Sarah, Caleb and I. Caleb threw sticks for Brutus, who brought them back along with big rocks and seaweed and whatever came up with the tide. We began to walk up the path again, Caleb carrying sticks, Sarah stopping to pick a hatful of rose hips. A fisherman pulled up lobster pots in the cove. Then, suddenly, Caleb straightened and looked past me to the top of the hill. He didn't speak, but his lips moved.

"What?" I asked him, and I turned to see a figure standing there, looking out at the sea.

Caleb's mouth opened and he dropped his sticks.

Papa. I leaned closer to hear him, and then he shouted.

"Papa! Papa!"

He began running up the hill calling Papa's name over and over. And I saw Papa turn at the sound of Caleb's voice. I ran, too, Sarah running behind me, and I began to cry.

"Papa!"

Caleb ran into Papa's arms and Papa held him close. Papa picked me up, too, and my hat fell off, and I buried my face in his neck.

Papa looked at Sarah.

"It rained," he said.

He smiled at her.

"I never thought you'd come," whispered Sarah.

"It rained," Papa said again, his voice so soft that it could have been the wind I heard.

Caleb sat on Papa's lap.

"And there were fireworks, Papa! Lots of them! How big are the kittens?"

"Big, like you," said Papa, smiling. He touched Caleb's face.

"Restless, like you."

"Do you want something to eat, Jacob?" asked Aunt Harriet.

"Harriet's solution to the problems of the world," said Aunt Lou, making Papa smile.

"No, thank you," said Papa. "I couldn't eat."

Caleb slid off Papa's lap. Papa stood, looking out over the water. No one spoke.

"That sound," Papa whispered after a moment.

"The sea," said Sarah.

Papa turned to look at her. She touched his arm and walked off down the path to the water. Papa looked at Caleb and me quickly;

then he followed her.

Caleb started to walk after Papa, but I reached out and took his hand.

"Caleb," I said softly.

"Where are they going?" Caleb asked.

"They'll come back," I said. "It's all right, Caleb."

Caleb and I stood and watched Sarah and Papa walk down the hill. They stopped. They talked. And then, after a moment, Papa put his arms around Sarah. I smiled.

"It's all right," I whispered to Caleb.

That night, after Aunt Harriet and Aunt Lou had played music for Papa, and Aunt Mattie had danced, we walked down by the water. And then Sarah and Papa told us that in the spring we would have a new baby.

"A real baby?" asked Caleb, excited.

"A real baby," said Papa.

"*Our* baby!" said Caleb, smiling.

Sarah saw my face and she knew I was worried. Worried because Mama had died when Caleb was born.

"It will be fine," she told me. "I am healthy. The baby's healthy. The doctor said so."

I looked at Papa.

"It will be fine, Anna," he said.

Clouds passed, and the full moon spread out over the water.

Papa put his arms around me.

"It will be fine. And it will be *wonderful*," he said.

15

"I see the house!" cried Caleb, standing up in the wagon. "And the new barn!"

The wagon passed the cornfields, still dry, but we could see some green in the meadow. We turned into our yard, and Nick and Lottie ran and jumped up into the wagon before it stopped.

"Nick, Lottie!"

I laughed as they jumped on us, licking our faces.

"There's some water in the pond," said Papa. He looked at Caleb and me. "And there are kittens waiting for you on the porch."

Caleb and I ran to the porch, where Seal washed her four kittens, three gray and one orange like Maggie's cat, Sam. Someone had left a bowl of water nearby.

"Look, Sarah!" Caleb held the orange cat for Sarah to see. She smiled at us, and then she and Papa began to walk out to the fields to see the green. I watched them, Papa dressed in his wedding suit, Sarah in her yellow bonnet. And then Sarah bent down suddenly, her traveling coat spread out behind her. She picked up a stick and began to write in the dry earth.

"What is she doing?" asked Caleb.

I knew, but I didn't say anything.

Papa turned and walked back to her, looking down at what she had written. She smiled up at him, and the two of them walked out into the fields in the late pale light of afternoon. Papa reached out and took Sarah's hand.

Caleb and I walked down the steps. Under the post where Caleb's glass still stood, Sarah had written one word in the prairie dirt.

Sarah.

Home.

It has rained twice. But there is still dust. The corn still rattles in the wind.

The green of Maine seems to be only a dream. When we came home by train, we passed trees and hills and lakes filled with water. They are beautiful, the trees and hills and lakes filled with water. But the prairie is home, the sky so big it takes your breath away, the land like a giant quilt tossed out.

It will rain again. There is some water in the pond. Not enough for swimming, but there will be. There will be flowers in the spring, and the river will run again. And in the spring there will be the new baby, Papa and Sarah's baby.

Caleb, like Papa, is not always good with words. But I think Caleb says it best.

Our baby.

Caleb's Story

ALSO BY PATRICIA MACLACHLAN

Sarah, Plain and Tall
Skylark
Arthur, For the Very First Time
Through Grandpa's Eyes
Cassie Binegar
Mama One, Mama Two
Seven Kisses in a Row
Unclaimed Treasures
The Facts and Fictions of Minna Pratt
All the Places to Love
What You Know First
Three Names

Caleb's Story

Patricia MacLachlan

For dear Pony,
with love
—P.M.

Caleb's Story

Anna has done something terrible. She has given me a journal to fill.

She wants me to write about the farm while she's gone, finishing school, working in town.

In Anna's journal the words walk across the page like bird prints in the mud. But it is hard for me. It is hard to find things to write about. Not much happens here, I told Anna. Chores, schoolwork, and more chores. Anna tells me I'll find something to write. Things to write about are all around you, she says.

I don't think so. There's only the cold, the skies as gray as goose feathers. And the wind. Always the wind.

—Caleb Witting

1

"Come find me, Caleb!" called my little sister, Cassie.

She ran out the door and down the steps. Lottie barked and followed her. Nick was older than Lottie. He stayed on the porch and watched.

"I don't have time. I mean it, Cassie!"

Cassie ignored me the way she always did when she wanted something.

"And don't look!" she called.

I sighed and walked after her. I covered my eyes with my hand, but through my fingers I could see Cassie run to the barn.

"One, two, three," I counted.

"Slower," she cried.

"Four . . . five . . . five and a half."

Papa was hitching Bess to the wagon.

"Don't be long," he said. "Anna's almost ready to leave."

"Don't worry. This won't take long, Papa."

"I don't know, Caleb. Cassie's getting better at hiding."

I laughed.

"At least you don't see her feet sticking out anymore. Six, seven, eight, nine, ten," I called.

I could hear Cassie laughing, but I couldn't see her. I walked into the barn. It was cool and dark and quiet. A winter sharp smell filled the space.

"Cassie?"

There was no answer. There was a time when Cassie would answer me and give away her hiding place—she couldn't help it. Not today.

May, my favorite of all our horses, was in her stall. I reached over and touched her nose, and she nickered at me. I could see her breath in the cold air. There was silence, the only sound the sound of May's breathing. Then I heard Lottie's bark outside, and Cassie's voice.

"Cassie? I hear you!"

I turned. Cassie tried to run by the barn door, and I rushed out and caught her, making her squeal.

"I've got you, Pal!"

Cassie laughed and we began to walk back to the house, Lottie leaping and jumping in front of us. Cassie reached up and took my hand, her face suddenly serious.

"There's a man."

"What man?"

"Behind the barn," said Cassie. "He's wrapped in a green blanket. He asked me about Papa."

I smiled.

"You and your imaginary friends, Cassie."

She scowled at me.

"There's a man," she insisted.

"You're stubborn," I told her. "Like Sarah."

"Like Mama," Cassie corrected me. "You could call her Mama."

"I could," I said. "But you know the story,

Cassie. When she first came here Anna and I called her Sarah. We will always call her Sarah."

"I will call her Mama," said Cassie.

I picked her up—she was so light—and Cassie put her head on my shoulder as we walked to the house.

"A man," she whispered in my ear.

"Do you have everything, Anna?"

Sarah wrapped biscuits in a towel.

"Give these to Sam."

Papa looked over Sarah's shoulder.

"Some," he said. "Not all."

Sarah smiled.

"Papa never gets enough biscuits," said Anna.

Anna tied up some letters with a long ribbon. Min, our orange cat, leaped up, trying to catch the ends. Her mother, Seal, slept in a basket by the fire, opening her eyes every so often to check on all of us.

"Justin's letters?" asked Sarah.

Anna nodded.

"I read them over and over," she said softly. "Sometimes I feel he's standing next to me."

Everyone was quiet. I used to tease Anna about her boyfriend, Justin. I called him Just-In-Time. But not anymore. Justin had gone to Europe to fight in the war. And no one teased Anna now. I think she worked for Doctor Sam because Justin was his son. It made her feel closer to Justin.

"Letters," said Papa, his voice low.

"You were the masters of letter writing, you and Sarah," said Anna.

"What does that mean?" asked Cassie.

"It means that they wrote letters to each other before they loved each other," said Anna.

"I never got to write letters," complained Cassie.

Papa smiled at her.

"No, you came much later."

"You came during an early snowstorm," I told Cassie, "with wind and snow and cold. I remember."

"We all remember!" said Anna, laughing.

"Did I come with letters?" asked Cassie.

"No," said Anna. "But you can write letters to me in town."

"I will," said Cassie, excited. "I will write you a hundred plus seven letters!"

"Here, Caleb," said Anna. She handed me some books.

"What is this?" I asked.

"My journals," said Anna. "And new ones. It is your job now."

"Mine?! I'm not a writer like you, Anna," I said.

"You'll figure it out, Caleb. One page at a time."

"I can't!"

"Everyone's not a writer, Caleb," said Anna. "But everyone can write."

Sarah looked out of the kitchen window.

"What is it, Sarah?" asked Papa.

"I thought I saw something. Someone, maybe. Over there."

Papa looked out, too.

"I don't see anyone. But I do see the

beginnings of snow. And the wind is picking up. Let's go!"

"Snow!" said Cassie. "And wind! Will someone be born?"

Sarah and Papa laughed.

"Not here," Sarah said. "Not tonight."

We picked up Anna's suitcase and packages and went out the door.

"She saw the man," whispered Cassie.

"Come on, Cass. There's no man," I said.

I took Cassie's hand and we went out where snow was coming down. Sarah looked worried.

"Anna? I want you to be careful. There's so much sickness."

"I know you worry about the influenza," said Anna.

"So many are sick," said Sarah, putting her arm around Anna. "So many have died. And you see the worst of it."

"I love working with Sam," said Anna. "You told me once that it is important to do what you love."

"I said that, did I?" said Sarah.

"You did," said Anna.

"You did," said Cassie, making Sarah laugh.

The snow was falling harder now, so that we couldn't see the clouds anymore.

"It's so early," said Sarah, pulling her shawl around her shoulders. "It shouldn't be snowing!"

"There are no rules for winter, Sarah," teased Papa. "This is the prairie, remember? Sometimes winter comes early. If the snow is heavy, I'll stay in town with Jess."

Sarah kissed Papa and Anna, and they climbed up in the wagon. Papa flicked the reins over Bess's back, and the wagon began to move off. Snow began to cover the ground.

"Anna!" I called suddenly.

Anna turned. I ran after the wagon.

"I'll write about winter!" I shouted.

Anna waved.

I stood, watching Papa's wagon wheels leave small tracks on the wet road. All around me was the soft surprising sound of snow falling. In the quiet, the prairie seemed larger than ever.

I'll write about winter.

And if I'm lucky, maybe something else will happen.

2

That afternoon something happened. Something that gave me more than schoolwork and chores and weather to write about.

Snow fell heavier during the morning, and I stayed home from school. It was hard to get home from school when there were storms. Once we had to stay all night in our schoolroom; sleeping close to the woodstove in our coats and hats and mittens; making our lunches last through the night; listening to the wind moaning around the corners of the school; listening to Mr. Willet, our teacher, snore.

When the wind grew stronger, Sarah sent me out to bring in all the animals—sheep from the west meadow, the cattle, and two of the horses. Cassie helped me herd the sheep. The wind blew Cassie's long hair loose from under her hat.

"Do we like winter?" Cassie asked.

I looked at her quickly. I could tell she wasn't kidding.

Cassie asked questions because she wanted to know the answers. Like Sarah. I looked at Cassie and she looked back at me, her eyes as sharp as Sarah's. My mother died when I was born, so I didn't know if I was like her.

"We like winter sometimes," I said.

She carried a bucket of grain in front of the sheep. They followed her as if she were their mother.

"I don't like this," Cassie said.

I opened the barn door and the sheep ran inside.

"You like to skate when the slough freezes over," I said to her.

Cassie smiled.

"I like that part of winter."

We closed the sheep pen. The smell of fresh hay filled the barn. Cassie sneezed.

"Now for the cows," I said.

Cassie frowned at me. I pulled her hand and we raced outside, out of the quiet of the barn into the wind, Cassie's hair flying out behind her like corn silk.

Sarah cooked soup on the stove, stirring it with a long-handled spoon. Cassie drew a picture at the table. I looked over her shoulder.

"What's that?" I asked.

"It's the man," she said firmly.

Sarah turned from the stove.

"What man?" asked Sarah.

"One of Cassie's imaginary friends," I told her.

Sarah looked at the drawing.

"That's lovely, Cass. And original."

"Lovely and original," said Cassie, imitating Sarah.

Sarah looked out the window.

"Caleb, you left the barn door open," she said.

"I closed it. I know I did," I said.

I put on my coat and went out. I ran my hand along the rope that we'd tied, one end to the house, the other by the barn door. When the storms were bad, anyone could get lost. A neighbor of ours had lost his way during a night storm and was found the next morning, frozen to death.

I looked in the barn, then stepped inside. Something was different. *Something.* May was there in her stall. The sheep bleated at me. Then . . . there was a horse in the next stall, Bess's stall. *It was a horse I'd never seen before.*

"What? Who are you?" I asked, reaching out to touch the horse. I heard a sound behind me and whirled around. There, slumped against the wall, was an older man, with gray hair. He was wrapped in a green blanket. He stared at me, but he said nothing.

"Who are you?" I asked. Then, gathering courage, "Where did you come from?"

The man didn't answer. He began to cough. I backed up.

"Wait!" I told him. "Stay here."

And I ran from the barn, calling Sarah's name over and over.

Sarah hurried after me to the barn, her coat flung around her shoulders.

"Who is he?" she asked.

I shook my head.

"He didn't say."

We opened the barn door and the man looked up at Sarah. She stepped inside and closed the door.

"Are you sick?" she asked. "There's influenza here. I have to protect my children."

The man shook his head.

"I'm not sick," he said, his voice low. "I'm cold. Cold to the bone."

Sarah reached out to touch his forehead briefly.

"You don't have a fever."

"No. I'm just cold."

Sarah paused, then made up her mind.

"Help me get him inside, Caleb," she said.

"There's no need," said the man. "I can rest here. In the barn."

"You'll do no such thing," said Sarah.

The man stared at Sarah for a moment. You could tell he thought about arguing with her. Then he reached out his hand to me. I helped him up, and Sarah and I walked him out of the barn and across the yard.

When we opened the door and walked into the house, Cassie stared at the man with her sharp, birdlike look. Sarah helped the man to a chair and put a quilt around him.

"There. That's warmer. Caleb? Get him hot tea from the stove, please."

I poured tea into a cup and handed it to the man. I studied him very carefully. We didn't have visitors at the farm very often, and never strangers. Cassie stood next to me.

"I told you there was a man," she whispered.

"Yes. You did," I said, my voice soft.

Seal got up from her basket by the fire and came over to sniff at the man.

His hands shook when he drank, and Sarah

helped him. He leaned back in the chair.

"That's good. Thank you."

"You're welcome. I'm Sarah Witting and these are my children, Caleb and Cassie."

"Cassie?" The man's face changed.

"And your name?" asked Sarah.

The man didn't speak for a moment.

"John," he said softly. "My name is John."

"Well, John, you are welcome to stay here. There's an extra bed upstairs because Jacob has taken our daughter, Anna, to town."

The man, John, sat up a bit.

"Jacob?" he asked.

"My husband, Jacob. Do you know him?" asked Sarah.

"Yes," he said, his voice low.

"Did you come to see him?" Sarah asked.

There was a silence.

"Yes," John said after a while. "Yes, I came to see him."

"He didn't say you were coming," said Sarah.

John took another sip of tea.

"He didn't know," said John.

Another silence.

"Caleb, John's tired. Please take him to Anna's room so he can rest," said Sarah.

I took John upstairs. He stood in Anna's room, looking around.

"My sister, Anna, is finishing school in town. And working for a doctor," I told him.

John nodded and sat down on the bed. He looked out the window, not speaking. He reached over and touched the table by the bed, a strange look on his face. Then he lay back on the bed, closing his eyes. I waited for a bit. Seal appeared in the doorway and jumped up on the bed beside John. She lay down.

"Seal," I whispered. "Get down."

But Seal only looked at me.

"I'm sorry about the cat. Her name is Seal. Do you want anything?" I finally whispered.

John said nothing. He was already asleep. Very quietly I left.

Downstairs Cassie was back at the table, drawing. Sarah folded clothes.

"Is he comfortable?" she asked.

I nodded. "Asleep. Seal is sleeping next to him."

"Really?" said Sarah, surprised. "Seal is very particular."

"Is he a robber?" asked Cassie.

Sarah smiled.

"If he is a robber, he isn't a very good one," she said. "He's sleeping."

I sat down and opened the empty book.

"If Anna were writing in this book," I said, "she would begin a story. 'Once upon a time a strange old man visited the Witting farm . . .'"

"A robber," said Cassie slyly.

"Stop that, Cassie. He is not a robber," said Sarah.

"Now I have something to write about in my book," I said.

"There are always things to write about," Sarah said. "Thoughts, fears, wishes, hopes, dreams."

I looked across the table at Cassie. Her mouth formed the word "robbers."

I smiled and began to write.

At last something has happened here. Not just snow and wind and chores. A strange man has come to the farm. Cassie found him first.

He is not imaginary.

But he is mysterious.

CW

3

The wind howled all afternoon, and when I looked out the window I couldn't see the barn. Cassie drew pictures by the woodstove, and Sarah read, stopping every once in a while to add vegetables to the soup. No sign of John.

"Should I go upstairs and check on him?" I asked Sarah.

"No, Caleb. Let him be. You could feed the animals, though."

I put on my coat and gloves.

"Remember the rope, Caleb," said Sarah, peering out the window. "You can't see a foot in front of you."

"I'll remember."

"And your hat, Caleb."

"Sarah!"

Sarah laughed and opened the door for me, and I went out into the wind and snow. There were already drifts, and I took hold of the rope, following it all the way across the yard, stumbling in the snow. The noise of the wind was so loud that I was surprised by the quiet of the barn when I stepped inside. I stood in the middle of the barn and looked all around. Papa had once said that the barn in winter was the most peaceful place he knew.

"It is a small peaceful place in the middle of a big land," he had told me.

It was true. No voices, only the animals, their breath and bodies so warm. I fed John's horse last, stroking his nose.

"Where did you come from?"

He stared at me, his eyes dark.

"And who is *he*?"

There was only silence in the barn. Papa was right.

The barn, so small in a big place.
Peace.

"John is awake," announced Cassie when I returned to the house.

"I can see."

John sat at the table, drinking tea. Seal sat at his feet. Min was now sleeping in Seal's basket.

"You look better," said Sarah.

"I am better," said John.

Cassie studied John closely. Finally he put down his cup of tea.

"What?" he said gruffly.

"Are you a robber?" asked Cassie.

"Cassie," warned Sarah.

"No," said John. "I am not a robber."

Sarah carried an armful of laundry upstairs. I opened my book.

"I'm writing about you," I told John.

John frowned.

"There is nothing to write about me," he said.

"But I have already written some things."

I pushed the book over for him to read.

John's lips were set in a thin line. He didn't even look at my book. He turned to Cassie, who had been staring at him all this time.

"Doesn't she do anything?" he asked me.

I smiled.

"She's little. She doesn't do much. She draws. She plays hide-and-seek."

"Hide-and-seek! Good idea. Go hide," he said to Cassie.

Cassie waited.

"You have to count," I said.

"Ah. One, two, three, four . . ."

"Slower," I told him.

John sighed.

"Fiiive, siiix."

Cassie ran off. John leaned back, looking pleased.

"There," he said. "She's gone."

He lifted his cup of tea.

"Ready!" called Cassie from somewhere in the house.

"Now you have to find her," I said.

"*You* go find her."

"I'm coming!" I called.

"Not you," came Cassie's voice. *"Him."*

John stared at his teacup. Then, muttering under his breath, he got up and left the room.

"I'm coming!" he called. "I'm coming," he repeated softly.

I looked at my open book. I wrote.

He didn't even look at it. Why wouldn't he look at what I wrote? Maybe he's afraid. But what is he afraid of?

We ate with the oil lamp throwing light across the table.

"Grace, Cassie?" said Sarah.

John stopped, his spoon halfway to his mouth. Cassie waited for him to put it down.

"God is great.

God is good.

And we thank him

For our fuud," said Cassie.

"Food," corrected Sarah.

"Foood," repeated Cassie.

John ate quietly, not looking at anyone. Especially Cassie.

John didn't look at Cassie, as if he knew what I knew. When you look at Cassie, she asks a question. Always.

This didn't work for John.

"Do you have children?" asked Cassie.

"Don't pry, Cassie," said Sarah.

"What does 'pry' mean?" asked Cassie.

"It means not poking into the life of someone who doesn't want it," said John briskly.

"But I want to know," said Cassie matter-of-factly.

"What I want is for you to eat your dinner," said Sarah sternly.

I smiled.

"Cassie makes me think of you, Sarah. When you first came here. You asked lots of questions."

Sarah smiled, too.

"I did, didn't I? And your father grew very tired of it. I came here from Maine," she told John. "After Jacob's wife died. Jacob wrote an advertisement in the newspaper for a wife. I read it. I came."

"And she stayed," I told John. "Anna and I were afraid she wouldn't. She missed the sea. But she stayed."

"That was a brave thing to do," said John.

"I thought so, too," said Sarah. "It seems a long time ago now."

"She brought Seal," said Cassie. "Now I'm here!"

"I'll say," said John.

Sarah got up and went to the window.

"I'm sure Jacob won't be home tonight. He'll stay in town. You can talk to him tomorrow, John."

John didn't answer. He took a medicine bottle out of his pocket when Sarah wasn't looking and took a pill. When he saw me watching, he quickly put the bottle back in his pocket. There was no more talk. No more questions.

The wind howls outside, the snow and sleet hitting the windows like stones tossed there. Inside it is peaceful. But John doesn't look peaceful at all. He looks like he has secrets.

I will find out what they are.

4

The morning was bright and clear when I woke, no snow or wind. I could smell coffee. John's room was empty. The bed was made, his small carrying pack by the window. I looked into Cassie's room and she was still asleep, one arm thrown back, her hair in a tangle.

Downstairs the coffeepot was hot to the touch. Through the window I could see John gathering wood from the shed. Nick watched and Lottie leaped through the drifts and barked. John tossed a small piece of wood and Nick picked it up. They began walking back to the house.

"Caleb? Did you make this coffee?"

Sarah was in her robe, a cup in her hand. I shook my head.

"It must have been John," I said.

The door opened and John came in with the dogs.

"This is wonderful coffee," said Sarah.

John nodded. "I've had years of coffee making," he said, dumping wood into the bin.

"That's Caleb's job, bringing in wood," said Sarah.

"Caleb took care of my horse yesterday," said John.

He sat down suddenly, his face pale.

Sarah looked alarmed. "Are you sure you're well enough for this?" she asked.

I wondered if John would tell Sarah about the pills he had hidden in his pocket, but he didn't.

John got up and poured coffee for himself.

"I'm well enough," he said quickly.

"The animals, Caleb. They need to be fed," said Sarah.

John held up his hand.

"No, Caleb. I've already done that."

"Thank you, John," said Sarah.

"I like this work," said John. "I used to farm a long time ago."

"Did you?" asked Sarah. "You know, I never asked you where you live, where your home is."

John took a long drink of coffee. He didn't answer. He looked over Sarah's head at Cassie on the stairs.

"Ah, the queen," he said.

Cassie came over and sat on Sarah's lap.

"The queen of what?" asked Cassie.

"Questions," said John. "The Queen of Questions."

Cassie smiled. She liked that.

The dogs sat up suddenly, listening. Lottie ran to the door and Nick followed her, barking.

"Hush," said Sarah, putting Cassie down. She went to the window.

"There's Jacob," she said, her face bright. "He's early!"

Sarah opened the front door, and cold air rushed into the warm kitchen. Papa came in and put his arms around Sarah.

"I'm glad you're home," said Sarah, her face in Papa's neck.

"I'm glad, too," said Jacob.

Very slowly John stood.

"Papa!" cried Cassie.

"There's my girl," said Papa.

He picked her up and came into the kitchen.

"Hello, Caleb."

"Is there school, Papa? Was anyone there when you went by?" I asked.

"No horses. I don't think there's school today," said Papa. "The snow has drifted pretty deep in places."

"Jacob, you have a visitor," said Sarah. "He came to see you yesterday."

"Oh?"

Papa looked at John.

"Do I know you?"

"You and I knew each other a long time ago, Jacob," said John.

Papa bent his head to one side thoughtfully. Then, as if he couldn't find any other words,

John repeated softly, "a long time ago."

Suddenly, Papa stepped backward as if he had been hit. He put Cassie down.

"Jacob?" asked Sarah. "What's wrong?"

Papa stared at John. Everyone was quiet. Even Cassie. When Papa did speak, his voice was so soft I could hardly hear him.

"You . . . ? How can it be . . . ?"

Papa's voice broke.

"Jacob? Jacob, who is this?" asked Sarah, stepping closer to Jacob as if to protect him from something. *What*?

Cassie moved closer to me and I took her hand. Then Papa saw us.

"Caleb. Take Cassie upstairs," he said sharply.

"Do you mean now?" I asked.

I was not used to his sharp tone.

"Yes, Caleb. Please get Cassie dressed," said Sarah more softly.

"Come, Cassie," I said.

"But Caleb—" Cassie began.

"Hush," I said.

Cassie and I went to the stairway, where we were out of sight. But Papa's voice stopped us, and we sat on the steps, listening.

"You were dead! Dead!"

Papa's voice sounded ragged, as if it hurt to talk. Startled, Seal ran past us up the stairs.

"Is that what she told you?" John asked softly.

"Jacob, who is this?" asked Sarah.

There was a moment of silence.

"This is my father. This is John Witting!" said Papa, his voice growing louder.

"But you told me he was dead," said Sarah.

I could hear the confusion in her voice.

"That's what I thought."

Cassie tugged at my sleeve.

"Who is he, Caleb?" she whispered.

"He is Papa's father. Our grandfather," I whispered back to her.

"Grandfather," whispered Cassie slowly, as if trying out a word she'd never used.

My heart began to beat so fast in my chest that I could hardly breathe.

Grandfather.

Then I heard the front door slam, Papa leaving. It opened and closed again. Sarah going after him. Then silence. I heard John walk across the kitchen and pull out a chair and sit down. Very faintly I heard the rattle of the pill bottle. My grandfather was taking a pill.

My grandfather.

5

From an upstairs window, Cassie and I watched Sarah and Papa talking outside. I had never seen Papa so upset. Maybe, once before, when he was afraid Sarah might not stay and marry him. But that had been a long time ago.

"Papa's mad," said Cassie.

She leaned against me.

"No, Cassie. He's upset. He thought his father was dead."

"Why isn't he glad to see him?"

Cassie looked up at me.

"Where has Grandfather been?"

I smiled at how natural the word "grandfather" was to Cassie.

I shook my head.

"I don't know."

"Maybe he was lost," said Cassie.

"Maybe."

"That's what happened," said Cassie firmly. "He was lost."

We watched Sarah talking to Papa. Papa stood silent, not even looking at her.

"Will everything be all right?" Cassie asked at last.

She sounded so sad.

"Everything will be fine," I said. "You'll see."

"I like Grandfather," Cassie said after a moment.

Cassie left, and I knew that she was going downstairs to ask Grandfather more questions.

"I like Grandfather, too," I said out loud in the empty room. "I do."

Outside, Sarah reached out and put her arms around Papa. But after a moment Papa walked off to the barn, leading Bess. Sarah stood still for a moment, then she pulled her coat around her and followed Papa into the barn.

I could hear Cassie's voice down in the kitchen, going on and on like the wind. Sometimes Grandfather would say something, his voice low, his sentences short. Slowly I walked down the stairs and into the kitchen.

"I am almost four and a half years old, you know," said Cassie.

"You told me that," said Grandfather.

"I was born here."

"So was I," said Grandfather grumpily.

"And I was very little," said Cassie.

"I was little," said Grandfather.

Cassie took a breath.

"I was *very* little. So little," said Cassie, "that I had to sleep in a little box by the stove. And I ate every hour. And I cried. And I threw up."

Grandfather grunted. "You win," he said.

"It will be nice to know my grandfather," I said.

Grandfather looked at me, his eyes so sharp and blue. He walked to the door and put on his coat.

"I'm not nice," he said. "Don't go thinking that, Caleb."

The kitchen door opened and Sarah came in.

"Why didn't you tell me who you were?" she said to Grandfather.

"I didn't know if I would be welcome in your house," said Grandfather.

"You are Jacob's father," said Sarah. "Of course you are welcome."

"Does Jacob welcome me?" he asked.

Sarah didn't answer. She walked to the stove to pour a cup of coffee.

"That's what I thought," said Grandfather. He put on his hat.

"Where are you going?" asked Sarah.

"Taking a walk," said Grandfather.

"I'll go with you," said Sarah.

"No," said Grandfather. "I know the farm. It was once mine, you know."

"I'll go," I said. "I'd like to."

"Aren't you late for school?" asked Sarah.

"There is no school," I said. "Remember?"

"Then help Jacob with the chores, Caleb."

"What about me?" asked Cassie.

Grandfather peered at all of us for a moment. Then he turned and went out the door.

"Grandfather doesn't like us," said Cassie.

"No. He doesn't," I said.

Sarah sighed and walked to the window to watch Grandfather walk down the road by the paddock fence.

"He doesn't know you," she said softly. "He will like you."

"Does he like Papa?" asked Cassie.

Sarah didn't answer.

"Does Papa like him?" asked Cassie.

Sarah turned from the window.

"Have you brushed your hair, Cassie? Chores, Caleb," she said briskly.

I knew there wouldn't be any more questions. Or answers.

Papa was in the barn, but he wasn't cleaning the stalls. He was standing in the open doorway, looking out over the meadows and the slough, filled with snow. He was also watching Grandfather walking down the road.

"Papa?"

Papa didn't answer me right away.

"The paddock gate needs fixing," he said, his voice soft.

"Papa? Cassie wonders . . ."

I stopped as Papa looked straight at me.

"Cassie wonders what?" he repeated.

I took a breath.

"Cassie wonders why you aren't happy to see your father. If you thought he was dead."

Papa knew I was asking for me, too.

"Cassie's life is simple, Caleb. She thinks life is good and fair. And everyone does the right thing."

We both watched Grandfather walk away down the road.

"But life *is* good and fair," I said. "Isn't it?"

Papa sighed.

"Sometimes, Caleb. But sometimes people do the wrong thing."

"Did Grandfather? Do the wrong thing?"

Papa winced at the name "grandfather." It did not come as easy for him as for Cassie.

Papa looked at me again.

"You know, Caleb, you're almost as tall as I am. When did that happen?"

Papa turned and walked back into the barn and picked up his shovel.

"The gate, Caleb," he said, his voice soft.

He bent over and began to clean out the stalls, his arms rising and falling in a regular rhythm. Up and down, up and down, up and down.

I mended the gate and looked up once to see Grandfather far away in the west meadow. When I looked up again he was gone. Later, when I went to the barn to put away the fence wire, Sarah and Papa were talking. They didn't see me and I didn't mean to listen. But I was afraid to move.

"You should talk to John," said Sarah. "Perhaps if you just talk about it—"

"That's your way, Sarah," interrupted Papa.

"I thought it was *our* way, Jacob."

Papa dropped his shovel and looked at Sarah.

"There is nothing to talk about. He walked away from us, Sarah. I was younger than Caleb. He walked away and left us to wait. And wonder." Papa's voice got louder. "Every day I looked down that road for him. *Every day!*" Papa was shouting now. "That shouldn't happen to a boy. That shouldn't happen to anyone."

Sarah put her arms around Papa.

"He's old and tired, Jacob. Please talk to him."

"What does he want after all this time?" asked Papa. "He could have written me a letter! Why didn't he write me a letter?" Papa's voice sounded sad.

Papa walked over to the barn door to look outside. He didn't see me in the shadows.

"I could forgive him for dying. But I will never, *never* forgive him for walking away," he said.

"Talk to him," whispered Sarah.

I stood still as a stone.

"You can tell him he can stay until he's well enough to go," said Papa.

"You can tell him that yourself, Jacob," said Sarah. "You are his son."

She walked out of the barn, past Papa, past me.

I stood quietly for a long time. Then, when I heard Papa begin to shovel hay again, I went out into the winter day.

Dusk came, and it was colder. Sarah and Cassie and I set the table for supper. Papa came in at last. He looked around.

Sarah shook her head.

"He hasn't come back from his walk."

Papa looked out the window. Daylight was nearly gone. Papa washed his hands.

"Is supper ready?" he asked.

"We can't eat without Grandfather!" said Cassie.

Papa dried his hands. He sat down at the table.

"We ate without him all these years," he said firmly. "We can eat without him tonight."

"I'll go look for him," I said.

"Caleb! Sit down!" Papa's voice was sharp.

I sat down.

"I think we should wait for him, Jacob," said Sarah. "He's our guest."

Papa stood up angrily.

"A guest! Of all things he is not . . ."

The door opened and Papa stopped. Grandfather came in and took off his coat, then saw Papa standing.

"Sorry to be late," said Grandfather. "I lost my way. It's been a long time . . ." His voice trailed off. "You should have eaten without me."

"That's what Papa said," said Cassie.

Grandfather looked at Papa.

"Your papa was right," Grandfather said.

Grandfather sat at his place. Papa sat, too.

"Grace, Caleb?" said Sarah.

"Thank you for our food," I said. "And thank you for friends who came to share it."

"That means you, Grandfather," said Cassie.

"I know, Cassie," said Grandfather softly. He turned to Papa. "I see you cut down a stand of trees in the west meadow, near the barn. Don't know if I would have done that. I fell out of one of those trees once," he said to me.

Papa said nothing.

"Do you like children?" asked Cassie, staring at Grandfather.

Grandfather took a spoonful of soup.

"Do you? Like children?" asked Cassie again.

Sarah reached out her hand and put it on Cassie's arm to stop her talk.

"Don't know many," said Grandfather.

"Do you like the ones you know?"

"No," said Grandfather.

Cassie was surprised at Grandfather's answer. Her mouth fell open.

"But what about Papa?" asked Cassie. "Did you like Papa when he was little?"

"Cassie! Eat," said Papa.

"But . . ."

"Hush," said Sarah.

Cassie was quiet for a moment. Then she looked at Grandfather.

"You are not a nice man," she said.

"Now, I told you that," said Grandfather.

No one spoke for the rest of the meal. Even Cassie was quiet. Lottie and Nick watched us, waiting for talk. But there was no talk.

"Good night, Grandfather."

I stood in the doorway of his bedroom. His oil lamp was burning. Grandfather stood by the window looking out.

"There's a moon," he said.

I went over and saw the moonlight on the barn, the meadows, the road going to town.

"I watched a lot of moons from this room," said Grandfather.

"You must have missed the farm," I said.

Grandfather was silent.

"You can read Anna's journals," I said. "There on the table. You can read all about the farm. And about us. While you were gone."

Grandfather didn't turn around.

I picked up one of Anna's journals and opened it. I began to read to Grandfather.

"'Papa married Sarah on a summer day. There were no clouds in the sky, and Papa picked Sarah up in his arms and whirled her around and around, her white dress and veil surrounding them like the summer wind. Caleb was so excited and happy, he burst into tears.

"'Everybody was happy.'"

There was silence, but Grandfather was looking at me.

"I did cry, I remember," I said. "And I was happy."

"Good night, Caleb," he said finally. "Close the door behind you."

Just before I closed the door, Seal crept into Grandfather's room and jumped up onto his bed.

Grandfather hasn't opened Anna's journals. He hasn't read mine. He doesn't talk to Papa. Only to Sarah, who makes him talk to her. Sometimes to Cassie and me.

I'm glad Grandfather came.

But I don't like the silence.

6

I didn't have to tell Sarah about Grandfather's pills after all. It was the dogs, Lottie really, who showed her in the end, and Grandfather running after Lottie all over the house. All that noise. The dogs.

There was no school for the next few days. The cold was hard for the horses and children. I would have liked it any other time, staying home. But not in this house. Not with Papa and Grandfather passing each other without talking, the only sounds in the house the clicking of

Sarah's knitting needles, Cassie's chattering, Min batting a marble across the floor. Two times I heard Sarah and Papa's voices, sharp and soft at the same time, behind their closed bedroom door. Once Papa had burst out of the room, brushing past me in the hallway. He had stayed in the barn most of the day.

"Why won't they talk to each other?" I whispered to Sarah.

"They are stubborn, Caleb."

"But they are family," I said.

"I know. That's what makes it so hard."

"Can't you do something? Can't you make Papa—"

"Caleb," Sarah interrupted me. "Your papa has to do this himself."

"I don't know, Sarah. Papa's angry. Will he hurt Grandfather?"

Sarah's look changed and she put her arms around me.

"Oh, no, Caleb. They are grown-up men. They won't do that. They will talk about their differences."

"Sarah?"

"Yes, Caleb?"

"I think Grandfather is sick."

Sarah looked at me closely.

"Why do you say that, Caleb?"

The door opened, and Grandfather came into the kitchen. The dogs followed, snow on their noses. Grandfather stamped his feet, leaving snow on the rug by the door. He sat down, the dogs surrounding him.

"They've adopted you, Lottie and Nick," said Sarah. "And Seal," she added as Seal jumped out of her basket and came over to Grandfather.

Grandfather was out of breath.

"Grandfather!"

Cassie came into the kitchen and leaned against Grandfather.

"I drew seven more pictures of you!"

She had dozens of pictures of Grandfather: Grandfather sitting, running, standing, sleeping, riding a horse (Grandfather was much larger than the horse), and Grandfather on the barn roof.

"Cassie has adopted you, too," said Sarah, smiling.

Grandfather looked at Cassie quickly, then away again, not inviting any questions from her. He stroked Lottie and Nick.

"We always had good farm dogs here."

Grandfather looked surprised at his own memory. Or maybe he was surprised he was talking about his memories.

"What kinds of dogs did you have?" I asked. "What were their names?"

Grandfather raised his eyebrows.

"You'll write about this, won't you."

"Maybe."

Grandfather looked at my journal on the table, then shrugged his shoulders. He leaned back in his chair.

"Pal was the big one, part hound, with long ears. She could jump over the tallest fences. Jacob . . ." He stopped for a moment. "Jacob used to try to get her to jump over the cattle."

"Did she jump over a cow?" asked Cassie.

"Don't know that," said Grandfather.

"And then there was Maudie," Grandfather went on. "She was small and black, like Lottie here."

Lottie wagged her tail at the sound of her name.

"Maudie loved winter. She would stay out all day, even in storms. We would have to go out and find her and bring her in at night. Then we found Rags one day, out in the slough, drinking water. He had wandered from somewhere far away. He looked like a heap of rags . . . thin and sorry lookin', but he was the sweetest dog of them all."

Grandfather looked at us, suddenly aware of the silence.

"Well," he said, embarrassed, "that was a lot of talk from me."

There was a small sound by the kitchen door. Lottie and Nick looked up, wagging their tails again. Papa stood there.

"Was that your dog, Papa? Rags who was sweet?" asked Cassie.

Papa didn't speak.

"Jacob?" asked Sarah, softly.

Then, as if waking from a daydream, and without a look at anyone, Papa went outside.

Sarah sighed. She went to the window and looked out.

Grandfather started to get up, then he sat down hard, his face showing pain. Sarah didn't see, but I saw. He put his hand on his chest. Then he took out his bottle of pills, but it dropped from his hand. Lottie, always hoping for play, picked up the bottle in her mouth and raced around the table.

"Lottie! Stop!" said Grandfather sternly.

But Lottie wanted to play. As soon as Grandfather got close to her, Lottie jumped back and raced away. Nick barked and ran after the two of them.

Finally, it was Sarah who stopped Lottie.

"Drop that," she said.

Lottie, who loved Sarah, dropped the bottle of pills at Sarah's feet.

"That is mine," said Grandfather.

Sarah looked at the bottle.

"What are these pills for, John?" asked Sarah. She turned the bottle around and read the label on the back.

"Heart? These are for your heart?" she asked.

"Where does it say that?" demanded Grandfather. "Where?"

I could see the words FOR HEART written on the bottle. Why couldn't Grandfather see those words, too?

"This is not your business," he added rudely.

"Yes it is," said Sarah carefully. "You are family. Your health is important to us."

Grandfather reached out for the bottle, but Sarah moved back.

"There are only a few pills left, John. We can drive to town and see Sam. He's our doctor."

Grandfather's face was still and angry.

"Those are my pills!" he said loudly.

"And you are *my* family!" said Sarah.

It was a contest of sorts. Sarah won, surprising Grandfather. Sarah, smaller than Grandfather, but just as fierce. Sarah won because it was decided—Sarah decided—that Grandfather would go to town in the wagon so he could see the doctor. Grandfather went upstairs, frowning. He was angry with Sarah.

Grandfather was lying on his bed, Seal next to his pillow.

"Grandfather?"

"I'm resting, Caleb."

"Don't be angry with Sarah, Grandfather."

"She shouldn't meddle in my business."

"Sarah has a strong mind," I said.

Grandfather made a small sound.

"Before Sarah came to the prairie, Papa was sad," I said. "Sometimes he didn't talk. He didn't sing. He had been alone for a long time.

Except for Anna. Except for me."

Grandfather turned away from me, facing the window. I picked up Anna's journal. "Anna wrote about that. About why Sarah made a difference in Papa's life. In our life."

I read.

"'Sometimes Sarah dances, and she makes Papa dance, too, his face shy, his smile like Caleb's smile.

"'Sometimes, when Papa worries about the farm or the weather, Sarah takes his hand and pulls him outside.

"'"Come, Jacob, come walk with me," she says.

"'And he does.

"'They walk the fields and the country road, Lottie and Nick following them. Once they chased each other through the rows of corn and we could hear the sounds of their laughter.'"

Grandfather didn't speak. But there was a sound behind me, Cassie in the doorway.

"Maybe *we* should dance," she said, her

voice small in the room. "Don't you think, Grandfather?"

Still, Grandfather didn't speak.

"Would that be good?" she asked.

After a moment I took Cassie's hand, and together, we left Grandfather alone.

7

The day was sunny, the sun on snow so bright that my eyes watered. Snow was melting. I could hear it dripping off the fences and the barn roof.

Papa was silent, his hands light on the reins. The wagon hardly made any sound on the snow-covered road. I sat in back with Cassie, Grandfather next to us, facing the farm, watching it disappear.

We passed the west meadow, Bess and May running alongside the fence with us, as if they wanted to go to town, too. We passed the slough, thick with ice. There were no clouds. The land stretched out so far that my eyes couldn't even see the places where the sky came down.

"Sing a song, Grandfather," said Cassie.

Grandfather ignored her.

"Please," said Cassie.

"I don't sing songs," said Grandfather.

"Never?" asked Cassie.

"Never."

"Never once?" asked Cassie.

Grandfather was quiet. But Cassie wasn't.

"Didn't you sing to Papa when he was a little boy?"

Very slowly Grandfather turned to look at Cassie. But before he could speak, Sarah cried out.

"Oh, no! Jacob, look!"

Sarah stood and Papa slowed the wagon.

A bonfire was burning in the cemetery. A family stood there next to the tiniest pine coffin I had ever seen.

"Jacob," said Sarah. "Stop. Please."

"Don't go over there, Sarah," said Papa. "It's the sickness."

"Stop the wagon," said Sarah.

Papa stopped and Sarah got down.

"What's wrong?" asked Cassie.

I put my arm around Cassie to protect her.

"Nothing important," I said.

"A fire to thaw the ground. To bury the dead," said Grandfather flatly. "By the looks of it, it's a baby who died."

Papa whirled around.

"Don't! It isn't your place to tell her anything," he said in a harsh whisper.

Grandfather stared back at Papa.

"I told her the truth."

I watched Sarah making her way through the snow to where the family stood. One of their children turned and watched her. And then the mother turned. Even from where we were in the wagon I could see the look of her. It made it hard for me to breathe, to see her face. Sarah put her arms around the woman.

Beside me Grandfather sat still. Cassie put her head on his shoulder. He didn't put his arm around her. But he didn't move away either.

Papa got down and went to meet Sarah. I could see she was crying. Papa took her in his arms and led her back to the wagon. Cassie began to cry, too, and Grandfather put an arm around her. Sarah and Papa climbed up in the wagon.

"We will stay together in town," said Sarah. "No wandering, Cassie. John will see Sam. Then we'll come straight home."

"But, Mama," protested Cassie. "I wanted to go to the store."

"No, Cassie," said Sarah. "You'll have to stay close to us."

Papa flicked the reins over the horses' backs. Slowly the wagon started off again, leaving us watching the fire burning, the small coffin, the family. We watched for a long time, until the fire became a tiny, faraway flickering light on the prairie.

There were not many people in town, only a few wagons and some cars. The streets looked lonely, and as we drove to Sam's office I could see pictures of flags hung in windows.

These families had sons who had gone to war in Europe. On other doors were black wreaths that meant someone had died there, of influenza or in the fighting.

"Caleb!"

Anna ran down the steps of Sam's house, smiling at us.

I climbed down from the wagon.

"I didn't know you were coming!" she said.

Papa and Sarah hugged Anna. Anna picked Cassie up.

"You're so big, Cassie! So tall!"

Slowly Grandfather climbed down from the wagon.

"Jacob?" said Sarah.

"This is John Witting, Anna," Papa said. "I'll take your list to the store, Sarah."

Sarah turned and watched Papa walk across the street to the store.

"John Witting?" Anna asked, curious.

Grandfather put out his hand.

"I'm your grandfather," he said bluntly. "You look like your papa. I've come to see the doctor."

Grandfather began to walk across the yard to the office.

Anna looked at Sarah.

"He's your papa's father," said Sarah.

"You can call him Grandfather," said Cassie.

"But Sarah . . . where has he been?" asked Anna.

Sarah shook her head.

"He's been lost," said Cassie.

Anna looked past the wagon, watching Papa go into the store.

"And Papa's not happy," she said.

"I wish you were home," I said to her. "You'd know what to do."

Anna turned.

"Wait. I'll take you in to the doctor," she called to Grandfather.

Grandfather waved his hand and climbed up the steps.

"I'll do this myself," he said.

Anna smiled.

"I was about to ask what he was like," she said.

"That's easy," I said. "He's like . . ."

"Papa," we said at the same time, laughing.

Sarah put her arm around Anna.

"You look tired. Are you getting enough rest? Have you heard from Justin?"

"I'm fine. I got a letter this past week. He's homesick."

Sarah sighed.

"First the war, then the influenza . . ." she said. "An early winter . . ."

"And then Grandfather," I said, making her smile.

"I like Grandfather," said Cassie. "He calls me the Queen of Questions!"

Anna laughed.

"Cassie will tell you all about him. She asks him questions from morning until night," said Sarah.

"And Caleb writes everything down in his journal!" said Cassie. "Someday I'm going to write everything down, too," she added.

"Heaven help us," said Sarah. She and Anna began to laugh.

Then Sarah's face was serious again.

"I want you to be very careful, Anna. We passed the Morgans . . ."

"Oh, their baby, I know . . ." Anna's voice trailed off.

Tears came to Sarah's eyes.

"I'm careful. It's getting better. It really is," said Anna.

Behind us the door opened and Grandfather came out, Sam behind him, frowning.

"Well?" asked Sarah.

Grandfather waved off her question.

"I'm fine. I'm fine. I don't want to talk about it," he said.

"He's a very stubborn man," said Sam.

"Is he all right, Sam?" asked Sarah.

Sam looked at Grandfather. Grandfather glared at Sam.

"I'm not allowed to talk about my patient, John Witting. It is confidential," said Sam.

"Confidential!" protested Sarah. "He's family, Sam."

Sam shrugged his shoulders.

"If he says it's private, it's private."

Papa came back then, a small box of groceries in his arms.

"Let's go," said Grandfather. "Time to go."

Grandfather climbed up in the wagon. Papa looked at Sarah.

"It's private," said Sarah crossly.

Sarah hugged Anna and got up in the wagon. Papa kissed Anna.

"I hope everything goes well with Justin," Sarah called to Sam.

"I hope so, too," said Sam, taking Anna's hand. "*We* hope so," he added.

The wagon started off.

"Take your medicine!" Sam called to Grandfather.

Grandfather didn't answer.

"Let me see your medicine, Grandfather," said Cassie.

Grandfather grunted.

"It's in your pocket," said Cassie helpfully.

Grandfather sighed and took two bottles out of his pocket.

"What does this say?" asked Cassie.

"I can't tell you," said Grandfather. "I don't have my eyeglasses."

Eyeglasses?

Cassie said what I was thinking.

"I never saw you with eyeglasses," she said. "Never once."

Grandfather leaned back and closed his eyes.

We rode home through the quiet, empty town in afternoon light. We passed the train station, where Sarah had gotten off the train, her first step onto our prairie, and we passed the granary. We passed the empty cemetery where the fire had died out. The sun went lower in the sky that spread out above us. The only noise was the sound of the horses' hooves. We came up the road and passed the slough and turned into our yard.

I looked at Grandfather.

What eyeglasses?

I pushed open the door to Grandfather's room.

Grandfather was folding his clothes on the bed, the two or three shirts he had brought, his worn pants.

"It's late, Caleb," he said. "You should be sleeping."

"You should be, too," I said.

"Good night then, Caleb."

Grandfather leaned over to blow out the oil lamp.

"Wait," I said. "Before you go to sleep I want you to read my book. I want you to read what I've written about you."

"Not now, Caleb," said Grandfather.

I took a deep breath.

"I'll read it to you, Grandfather," I said.

I opened my book. I began to read to him.

"'I love that Grandfather has come to our farm. *His* farm. I love having a grandfather who will teach me about a time I never knew. Someone who can tell me that he had a sweet dog, Rags, and that once he fell out of a tree in the west meadow. Someone who will teach me about Papa.

"'I know a secret about Grandfather.'"

I looked up at Grandfather. He stared at me.

"'I know that Grandfather doesn't wear eyeglasses. I know why he doesn't read my journal, Anna's journals. I know why he never wrote a letter to Papa when he went away.'"

I stopped. I felt tears at the corners of my eyes.

"You don't know how to read, Grandfather, do you?" I said very softly, almost whispering. "So you didn't know how to write a letter to Papa."

Grandfather didn't say anything. I moved closer to the bed and showed him my book.

"You can learn," I said. "You can."

"That's enough, Caleb," he said.

Grandfather moved to the window. He stared out into the dark.

"I'm too old," he said more softly.

I went over and took Grandfather's hand.

"Grandfather," I said, looking up at him. "I am going to teach you."

8

There was school, day after day after day. I rode Bess the two miles there and back. I carried my notebook with me in my pack, writing in it at recess and lunch, sometimes writing in it when I was supposed to be doing other work. There were twelve of us in our one-room schoolhouse, ages six to fifteen. We all helped each other. Sometimes the older ones helped the younger ones. I taught Lily how to read. But sometimes the younger ones helped the older ones. Joseph was good at addition and long division. He was only nine, but he was the best at figures.

I depended on Cassie for news at home during the day.

"What happened today?" I whispered.

"Nothing. It's too quiet here, Caleb. Only Min plays with me. Stay home from school. Please."

"I can't do that, Cassie."

"Papa doesn't play games with me. He works in the barn all the time."

"What about Grandfather?"

"Grandfather takes walks. Sometimes he talks to Sarah. He stays in his room."

"What does he do there?"

"I don't know. Maybe he reads," said Cassie.

"I don't think so, Cassie," I said.

It was hard to escape Cassie. She wanted to play. She wanted me to read books to her. She wanted to skate in the slough with me when the snow had been cleared. But every evening I went up to Grandfather's room and shut the door. The next two weeks, in secret, we read nearly all of Anna's journals, so Grandfather knew about our lives without him. Grandfather learned quickly, as if he had been ready for this.

"'Dear Mr. Jacob Witting,'" read Grandfather

haltingly, slowly. "'I am Sarah Wheaton from Maine . . .'"

He looked at me.

"That was her first letter to Jacob?" he asked.

I nodded.

"The answer to Papa's advertisement for a wife and mother," I said. "And then she wrote to us. See, there."

I pointed, and Grandfather began to read.

"'My favorite colors are the colors of the sea, blue and gray and green, depending on the weather.'"

Grandfather sat back.

"She came a long way."

"We were excited," I said. "Sarah wrote that she was coming. And then she added something for Anna and me that made us even more excited."

"What?" asked Grandfather. "What did she write?"

I turned the pages of the journal.

"There," I said. I couldn't help smiling.

"'Tell them I sing,'" read Grandfather.

He couldn't help smiling either.

"We were afraid she wouldn't stay," I said. "She loved Maine."

Grandfather nodded. He closed the book that Anna had written so long ago. I could tell our lesson was over for today. Grandfather walked to the window and looked out over the farm.

"You always love what you know first," he said. "Always," he repeated softly.

On Saturday there were clouds in the sky. The air felt damp and raw. I knew it would storm again.

It was stormy in the house, too. Papa came in for meals, but spent most of his time working: fixing fences, shoveling out stalls and putting down new hay, making sure the barn was strong enough for winter winds. Grandfather took long walks and once helped Sarah cook a stew. Sarah loved Papa and she liked

Grandfather, but I could tell she was upset with them both for not talking. Cassie talked for everyone. And it was Cassie who caused the trouble.

We ate an early supper, the wind outside whining around the corners of the house, the candles on the table flickering.

"When I was born," said Cassie suddenly, "Mama and Papa named me Cassie. That was my grandmother's name."

Everyone was still.

"Grandfather knows that, Cassie," I said softly, warningly. "Grandmother was his wife," I whispered.

Papa didn't look up. He kept eating his stew.

Grandfather looked at Cassie and surprised us by smiling.

"Your grandmother would have liked you, Cassie," he said. "That is one thing I know."

Papa stood up, his chair crashing to the floor behind him. Cassie's fork clattered to her plate.

Papa's face was dark, and I don't ever remember seeing him so angry.

"You!" he said to Grandfather. "You know nothing. *Nothing!* You, of all people, cannot speak for my mother."

"Jacob," said Sarah. "Not here. Not now."

"Yes, now!" Papa shouted. "Why shouldn't Cassie and Caleb know what he is really like? That he left us. That he walked away!"

Cassie burst into tears. Sarah stood, her face as angry as Papa's.

"Not in front of the children, Jacob. Don't do this."

Grandfather got up and walked to the door.

"Sarah's right, Jacob. Not here."

"Don't you tell me what is right. Not you. Ever!" said Papa angrily.

Grandfather put on his coat and went out into the wind.

After a moment, Papa followed, slamming the door behind him.

There was silence, except for Cassie's crying.

Sarah took Cassie on her lap. I got up quietly. I went to the door and put on my coat. Sarah watched me, over Cassie's head, her face sad and scared, but she didn't stop me. I went out the door. I walked across the snowy yard, the wind tearing at my clothes, snow crunching under my feet. There was no moon.

The barn door was half open. I could hear Papa's and Grandfather's voices. I crept inside.

"I want to know why you're here," said Papa loudly. "Why did you come back?"

I peered around a stall and saw Papa come close to Grandfather.

"Sometimes . . ." Grandfather began. "Sometimes you want to see how things are. How things turned out."

"Well, there are things you never saw! Things you couldn't know!" said Papa. "I waited for you! Every day I looked down that road . . . waiting to see you."

I was afraid to move.

"Things were different than you think, Jacob," said Grandfather.

"Different how?" shouted Papa. "Different than your leaving? Than Mama's crying?"

"Yes, different," said Grandfather.

"Why didn't you write me a letter?" asked Papa. "You never even wrote to me."

I wanted to cry out "He couldn't! Grandfather couldn't!" But I said nothing.

Papa turned to look at Grandfather.

"I loved you!" he cried. "And I waited for your letters."

And then it happened. Papa pushed Grandfather and Grandfather pushed back. Hard. Papa fell back over the plow and lay still.

"Jacob?" said Grandfather.

Papa didn't speak.

Grandfather knelt down next to Papa.

Papa moaned.

"My leg. It's my leg . . ."

"I'll get help, Jacob. Stay still," said Grandfather.

"Sarah! Caleb!" Grandfather shouted. "Help me!"

I ran through the dark yard, where snow and sleet pounded at me. Wind caught the door as I opened it, bringing in snow and wind. Sarah turned from the sink, her smile slowly fading as she saw my face. When we both ran back to the barn and helped Papa to the house, the worst had happened.

Papa was hurt.

And a storm had come.

9

Papa lay on the bed, his face so pale. Cassie cried, and Papa held out his hand to her.

"It's all right, Cassie. I'm fine," he said.

"How did this happen?" asked Sarah. "How?"

Papa looked at Grandfather and sighed.

"I fell," he said. "I fell in the barn."

Grandfather leaned over and ran his hands over Papa's leg. Papa caught his breath in pain.

"It's broken," said Grandfather.

Papa moaned again, and Sarah put a cool washcloth on his head.

"I'll go get Sam," I said.

Sarah looked out the window.

"It's too fierce outside," said Sarah. "You can't go."

Sarah looked at Grandfather.

"And you won't go, either," she said. "What should we do?"

Grandfather pushed up his sleeves.

"I'll set it," he said.

"You?" said Sarah.

"I've done it before. But I'll need help," said Grandfather.

No one spoke. Sarah took Papa's hand. He closed his eyes.

"Do it," Papa said softly. "Do it."

"I'll need two poles the length of Jacob's leg," said Grandfather quickly. "And strips of cloth to tie them."

"In the shed, Caleb," said Papa, his voice sounding weak.

"Get them, Caleb," said Sarah. "Hurry. I'll get the cloth."

I ran out into the storm. The wind almost blew me over, and I felt sudden ice under my eyes. I knew I was crying.

Lottie and Nick sat up and watched me when I came back into the warm kitchen. I carried two poles.

In the bedroom, Cassie climbed up on the bed. Papa cried out with pain.

"Cassie," said Grandfather very softly and carefully. "I need you to do something for me. For your papa. I want you to go hide. I will come and find you later."

Cassie stared at Grandfather.

"Do you promise?" she asked.

"I promise."

"Now?"

"Right now," said Grandfather. "One, two, three . . ."

Cassie ran out of the room.

"Four, five . . ."

"Slower," said Papa softly.

"Six . . . seven . . ." said Grandfather more slowly.

"Sarah, I want you to hold Jacob from behind," said Grandfather. "And hold him no matter what. Even if he tells you to stop."

Sarah nodded.

Grandfather took my arm.

"I want you to go with Cassie. She'll need you."

"Now?" I asked, echoing Cassie's question.

Grandfather smiled at me.

"Now," he said.

I went to the door and looked back once. Papa's eyes were closed. Sarah got up on the bed behind him. Grandfather looked at me. A sudden burst of wind tossed sleet and snow against the window. I left the room.

I fed Lottie and Nick. Seal and Min slept together in the basket. Then I put wood in the stove and sat down at the kitchen table. The kitchen was dark and dreary, and I shivered. I saw something move, and Cassie peeked out from under the daybed.

"I'm waiting for Grandfather," she whispered.

"You may have a long wait, Cassie."

Then, before Cassie could answer, there was a terrible cry from the bedroom. *Papa.* And then another cry. Cassie scrambled up and climbed into my lap. I held her, and she buried her face in my neck. We sat there as the room grew darker, and the wind blew snow against the house, and the dogs came to lean against my legs.

"Caleb?"

Sarah woke me late. I was sleeping at the kitchen table, my head on my arms.

"Papa . . . ?"

"Papa's fine. He's sleeping. John did a good job."

Grandfather came into the kitchen.

"I hope I never have to do that again," Sarah said.

Grandfather nodded and poured a cup of coffee.

"Me, too," he said. "You were a good help, Sarah."

Grandfather sat down, rubbing his eyes.

Sarah smiled.

"But you did it," she said.

It was quiet in the kitchen, the wind suddenly dying outside.

"Jacob. I remember once . . . when Jacob

was very little," said Grandfather, "he got his hand caught in a bridle and broke his finger. He never complained."

The wind came up again, a sudden burst rattling the windows.

"Where have you been all this time?" asked Sarah so softly that her words were almost lost in the room.

Grandfather looked at her.

"Everywhere but home," he said, just as softly.

"I'm glad you're here now," said Sarah.

"I'm glad, too," I said.

"It was my fault, though," said Grandfather. "What happened to Jacob."

"It could have been you with a broken leg," I said. "Papa pushed you, too."

Sarah smiled.

"You two," Sarah said to Grandfather. "You and Jacob. How alike you are."

"Who am *I* like?" I asked.

"Who do you want to be like?" asked Sarah.

I thought about that. I had thought about it for a long time, but I didn't say anything.

"Where's Cassie, Caleb? Is she asleep?" asked Sarah.

Grandfather smiled. He leaned over and took Cassie's foot, sticking out from under the daybed.

"I found you, Cassie," he whispered. "I found you."

10

I thought things would be better between Papa and Grandfather, but they weren't. Papa was silent in his room. Grandfather and I mended fences and fed the animals and shoveled out stalls.

"What's your horse's name?" I asked Grandfather.

"Jack," said Grandfather.

"Papa had a horse named Jack, too," I told him.

Grandfather didn't answer.

"Sarah's right. You and Papa are alike," I said.

I knew Grandfather wouldn't answer. And he didn't.

"And Jacob didn't go to Maine when the

drought was here?" Grandfather asked me. We were in his room, the door closed.

"He stayed here. Alone," I said. "Until the rains finally came. And then he came to Maine, surprising us all. But he was the one who was surprised, because Sarah and Papa had Cassie after that. And she was the biggest surprise of all."

I pointed to what Anna had written.

"'When we came home by train, we passed trees and hills and lakes filled with water,'" read Grandfather.

Grandfather could read better now, his voice strong.

"'They are beautiful, the trees and hills and lakes filled with water. But the prairie is home, the sky so big it takes your breath away, the land like a giant quilt tossed out.'"

Grandfather closed the book. It was very quiet in the room.

A knock at the door made us both jump.

"Hello? Are you in there, Caleb?" asked Sarah.

"Yes. I'll be down soon," I called to her.

"What are you doing? Is John there?"

"Yes, Sarah," said Grandfather. "We're almost done."

"It's private," I said.

There was silence behind the door. Soon we heard Sarah's footsteps going down the hall and down the stairs.

I handed Grandfather a blank book.

"What is this?" he asked.

"This is yours," I said. "Yours to write in. You can do it now."

Grandfather opened it. I had written his name—JOHN WITTING—there. He turned the pages and saw them all empty and white. Grandfather put a hand on his chest.

"Grandfather?"

I was scared. I thought he was sick.

Grandfather waved me away.

"It isn't pain," he said to me.

He closed his empty book and looked at me.

"It's love," he said.

When the weather cleared, Sam came out to the farm. He taught Papa how to use crutches so he could get around. Then he gave Grandfather a lecture I wasn't meant to hear. I was in the hallway, out of sight. Sam and Grandfather sat at the kitchen table.

"You can't do all the work, John," said Sam. "Your heart can't take it."

"Nonsense," said Grandfather.

"Oh, I see," said Sam. "You feel guilty for leaving Jacob when he was little. So you'll make up for it by working hard and dying. That will make things right again?"

"More nonsense," said Grandfather. "Want some more coffee? I made it."

Sam shook his head.

"Stubborn," he said. "Old fool."

Papa came into the kitchen on his crutches, Sarah and Cassie with him.

"Easy, Jacob," said Sarah.

She helped Papa to a chair.

"I can do this," said Papa. "It is good to be out of bed."

"No work, Jacob," said Sam. "I mean that."

"Grandfather and Caleb are doing the work," said Cassie, sitting on Grandfather's lap.

Sam frowned.

"So I hear," he said. "Is that true, Sarah?"

"There's been a lot of repair work from the storms," said Sarah. "I don't know what Caleb and I would do without John."

Sam frowned at Grandfather. Grandfather ignored him.

"Any letters from Justin?" Sarah asked Sam.

"No letters for a while. Anna waits for the mail every day."

"Are you worried?" asked Sarah.

Sam got up and put on his coat.

"Yes, a little. Letters take such a long time."

"And the influenza?" asked Papa.

"Better, Jacob. Fewer cases. I think it has run its course," said Sam.

"We think about Justin every day," said Sarah.

"Thoughts are good," said Sam with a smile. "Having him here would be better."

Sam went to the door and turned.

"No work, Jacob. And"—he looked at Grandfather—"you know what I think."

"What does that mean?" asked Sarah.

"It's—" Sam began.

"Private," said Sarah and Sam at the same time.

It was evening. Sarah was in the bedroom with Papa. He was tired from learning to use his crutches. Grandfather was tired, too. We had replaced a barn beam. It had taken a long time.

I worry about Grandfather. Sam says his heart cannot take much work. I try to keep him from shoveling hay, from cleaning out the stalls. I try to keep him safe. But winter is hard here. Winter makes you tired. Even walking through the snowdrifts makes you tired.

In the kitchen, Cassie sat on Grandfather's lap.

"What now?" asked Grandfather.

He sounded gruff, but Cassie knew better. Cassie wasn't afraid of Grandfather.

"Would you sing me a song?" asked Cassie.

"I don't know any songs," said Grandfather.

"Yes, you do," said Cassie. "I heard you humming a song when you were in your bedroom. When the door was closed. I was outside, listening."

"Were you?" said Grandfather with a small smile. "What song?"

Cassie hummed a little of a song.

"Did I hum that?" said Grandfather. "That was a long time ago. Too long ago for me to remember the words."

Cassie didn't say anything. She stared at Grandfather for a long time. Finally, he gave in.

"Oh, all right," he said.

"Don't you laugh," Grandfather warned me. "Don't even smile."

"Okay."

And then, in the dark room, Cassie on his lap, Grandfather began to sing.

"Sleep, my love, and peace attend thee,
All through the night;
Guardian angels God will lend thee,
All through the night.
Soft the drowsy hours are creeping.
Hill and vale in slumber steeping,
I my loving vigil keeping,
All through the night."

I looked up and saw Sarah standing in the doorway, Papa behind her on his crutches. Sarah smiled at Cassie, her head on Grandfather's shoulder. But Papa didn't smile. He looked odd. He looked sad. He looked like someone remembering something that he hadn't thought of for a long time.

"Angels watching ever round thee,
All through the night;
In my slumbers close surround thee,

All through the night.
They should of all fears disarm thee,
No forebodings should alarm thee,
They will let no peril harm thee,
All through the night."

When I looked up again, Papa had gone. Sarah's eyes were wet from tears.

"Again," whispered Cassie. "Sing it again."

I stood outside Sarah and Papa's bedroom. I raised my hand to knock, then stopped. I could hear voices inside the room. Sarah and Papa's voices.

"John has done so much, Jacob," said Sarah. "He—"

"Sarah, I know what you're trying to do. I told you once, and I'll say it again: I will not forgive him!"

There was a silence, then Sarah's voice, sounding soft and hard at the same time.

"Your unforgiving nature is something I do

not love about you, Jacob," she said softly.

Papa didn't answer her. And suddenly the door opened. Sarah looked at me for a moment, then she brushed by me without saying a word.

Papa just stood there inside. I had never ever heard Sarah say she didn't love *anything* about Papa.

Sarah has always loved Papa. What will happen to us if Sarah doesn't love Papa anymore? Sarah is sad, I know. I see her face when she looks at Papa. Sarah's sad.

But Papa's just angry.

"Papa?"

Papa turned from the window and sat on the bed.

"What is it, Caleb?"

"My birthday is coming," I said.

"Yes, it is," said Papa.

"And I don't want books or tools or even a horse of my own for my birthday."

Papa looked up, surprised.

"You've always wanted a horse of your own, Caleb."

"Not this year," I said. "What I want this year is something different."

"Different?" repeated Papa.

I nodded.

"This year I want most of all for you to forgive Grandfather. I want you to forgive Grandfather so I can grow up and be just like you," I said.

Papa stared at me. He said nothing. He lay back on the bed, and, after a moment, I went away. I closed the door behind me.

11

Another storm came. I retied the rope to the barn. The horses had been restless, a sign there would be bad weather, and the dogs paced.

"Don't fret, Lottie," said Grandfather. "We'll keep the fire going and feed you well. Your life is good."

"Their lives are good, aren't they?" I said. "They have no worries."

Grandfather smiled.

"What worries do you have, Caleb?"

I shook my head, not wanting to talk about it. I had seen Grandfather's bag packed. I had seen Papa pass Grandfather in the hallway, neither of them speaking. I had heard Sarah's words to Papa, the words telling him what she did not love about him.

"Are you worried about your papa?" Grandfather asked.

I felt tears in my eyes. Grandfather put his arms around me. I looked over to the house, and I could see Papa watching us through the window.

"Your papa will be fine soon, Caleb. He gets stronger every day. Pretty soon he'll only use a cane. He'll be happy when he's working again."

"I'm not worried about his leg, Grandfather."

My throat felt tight.

"Ah," said Grandfather. "Look, Caleb. Your papa has reason to be angry with me. I did a very bad thing years ago. I did something that affected his life. Every single day of it."

"But you can write him a letter now," I said.

Grandfather sighed.

"I can, Caleb. But don't go thinking it will make everything better with your papa."

Grandfather went to feed the horses. I looked to the house, and Papa was still there, his face in the window, watching Grandfather and me.

Above us the sky darkened.

A noise woke me in the middle of the night. Was it the wind? Or was it the kitchen door closing? Snow blew against my windows, and I went down the stairs and into the kitchen. An oil lamp burned on the table. Lottie stood by the door, wagging her tail.

"Lottie? What's the matter? Where's Nick?"

Lottie whined and jumped up on the door. I looked out the window, but I couldn't see anything in the storm.

"Sarah?" Papa called softly from the bedroom.

"No, Papa. It's me. Caleb."

I heard Papa get out of bed. He came into the kitchen slowly.

"Where is she?" he asked. "She was going to call Nick. He didn't come in. Sarah was worried."

Papa came closer to me.

"Caleb? Where is she?"

My heart seemed cold. Cold like the wind outside.

"Her coat is gone. She wouldn't go out in this, Papa. She always told me never—"

Papa called up the stairs.

"Sarah? Are you there?"

There was only silence. Lottie began to howl.

"Sarah!" His voice sounded frightened.

Grandfather came down the stairs, his hair sleep-mussed.

"What's wrong?" he asked.

"Sarah," said Papa. "She's out in this."

Papa went over on crutches to get his coat.

"No," said Grandfather. "You're not strong enough yet. Not fast enough. I'll go."

Grandfather put on his coat and boots.

"She went after Nick," I said.

"Her coat is red," said Papa. "Look for a red coat."

"Don't worry, Jacob," said Grandfather. "The rope is up. I'll take Lottie with me."

Grandfather took the lamp from the table.

"I'll come with you," I said.

"Stay with your papa," he said. "Lottie will help."

The door opened, wind and snow blowing in. Then the door closed again and it was quiet.

"I should go," I said to Papa. "Grandfather's sick. He's not supposed to go out in this."

"What do you mean?" asked Papa.

"I heard Grandfather talking to Sam. Sam told him he'd die if he worked too hard. I want to go, too."

I stopped talking and began to cry. Papa put his arms around me and held me. We stood that way for a long time as the wind howled. Then the door opened suddenly, Nick and Lottie bounding in.

"Caleb," said Grandfather quickly. "I need you. Now! We have to dig Sarah out of the snow."

"Is she all right?" asked Papa.

"I don't know," said Grandfather softly. "Caleb?"

Together we went out into the storm.

"The rope broke," shouted Grandfather. "I found her by the tree. Nick was with her."

We struggled through the snow and wind. I could barely see Grandfather in front of me. And then I saw a little bit of red in the snow. Sarah was buried there, her face almost the color of snow.

"Sarah!" I shouted.

"She can't hear you, Caleb!" shouted Grandfather. "Here, help me dig her out."

We used shovels and our hands until we could half carry, half lift Sarah out. She was so limp. I was so afraid.

When we opened the door, Papa's face looked as pale as Sarah's.

"Sarah!" he cried out.

"Talk to her, Jacob. Try to wake her. Don't let her sleep," said Grandfather.

We lay Sarah on the daybed. Grandfather covered her with blankets and took off her boots.

"Get some tea, Caleb. Or coffee. Anything hot," he said.

"Sarah," said Papa, his voice frightened.

He touched her face.

"Sarah!" he said louder, frantically. "Don't sleep. Don't sleep!"

I handed Papa a cup of tea. Papa raised Sarah's head and spoke softly to her.

"Sarah, drink this now. We want you to wake up. Now, Sarah. Please!"

Suddenly, Sarah's eyes opened.

"Nick," she said, her voice faint.

Papa smiled. Tears came down his face.

"Nick's fine, Sarah," said Papa. "Here, Nick."

Nick went over to Sarah and nosed her hand. Sarah's eyes closed again.

"It was cold. So cold," Sarah said, confused. "And I was so tired."

Grandfather rubbed Sarah's feet.

"It's all right, Sarah," said Grandfather.

"And the rope broke," said Sarah.

Papa took Sarah in his arms.

"It's all right, Sarah."

Papa looked at Grandfather and at me.

"You're fine. Everything is all right now," he said.

Grandfather took off his coat and boots. He went up the stairs to bed, walking slowly. After a while I left, too. Left Papa rocking Sarah while Lottie slept, and Nick sat watching Sarah while the wind howled outside.

12

I didn't remember the wind dying in the night. I didn't remember falling asleep. When I woke it was light, the sun high, shining on the iced trees. The fence around the paddock looked slick and cold. From my window I could see the horses' cloud breaths as they ate hay.

Cassie's room was empty, her bed rumpled. Grandfather's room was neat, his bed made. Next to the door stood his bag, all packed. The journal I had given him sat on top.

I ran down the stairs, stopping suddenly in the kitchen. Grandfather and Sarah sat at the kitchen table, drinking coffee. I could hear Cassie chattering to Papa in his bedroom.

Sarah smiled at me.

"Sleep well, Caleb?"

I shook my head.

"What happened last night was my fault," I said. "I put up the rope, Sarah. I must have done it wrong."

"Fault?" said Sarah. "Oh, Caleb, I want you to listen to me. There comes a time when fault doesn't matter. Things happen. And we can't blame ourselves—or someone else—forever."

I heard a noise behind me, and saw Papa standing there, Cassie beside him. I knew he had heard Sarah's words.

"Look," said Cassie. "Papa's using a cane now."

Papa sat down at the table. Grandfather poured him coffee.

"You must have been up all night," he said to Papa.

Papa looked at Sarah.

"I didn't want her to go back to sleep," he said.

Grandfather smiled.

"No, you didn't."

Grandfather stretched.

"I have some things to finish before . . ." He stopped.

He looked at us for a moment, then he walked up the stairs.

"Before what?" asked Cassie.

"Before he leaves," I said quickly. "His bag is packed upstairs. He told me that soon you could go back to work, Papa. That you'd be happier then."

Papa looked toward the stairs.

"I don't want Grandfather to go away," said Cassie. "I don't."

Her eyes filled with tears.

"Cassie," said Sarah softly. "Please make your bed."

"Do I have to?" said Cassie.

Sarah smiled.

"All right," said Cassie.

She ran off, her shoes clattering on the wooden stairs.

Sarah looked at me, and I knew what her look meant. I should leave them alone, too. I took a biscuit and started up the stairs.

"Things happen, Jacob," I heard Sarah say. "The rope broke. I could have died."

"Don't, Sarah," said Papa.

"You could have lost me, Jacob," said Sarah. "And that's the way life is. Something happens . . . one little moment in time. If you're lucky, you have a chance to make things better. You have that chance here. Don't let it pass."

I heard Papa get up from his chair.

"Do you want some help?" asked Sarah.

"No," said Papa. "I'll do this myself."

I walked up the stairs quietly, Papa slowly coming up the stairs behind me. Grandfather stood at his window, looking out over the farm. As if he didn't even see me, Papa passed me and went into Grandfather's room. Grandfather and Papa, so much alike, faced each other.

"Jacob?" said Grandfather. "Sit down."

Papa shook his head.

"I'm all right. I'll stand," said Papa, leaning on his cane.

There was a long silence. Then came Papa's voice, softer than I'd heard it in a long time.

"Why didn't you take me with you? All those years ago. I wanted to be with you. No matter where you were."

"Jacob—" said Grandfather.

But Papa went on.

"You didn't write. Not one letter. And I waited and waited."

"I know," said Grandfather. "I couldn't write, Jacob, because . . . I didn't know how to write you. I never learned."

Papa moved closer to Grandfather.

"I was so ashamed," whispered Grandfather. "Caleb knew. Caleb taught me. All the evenings in this room, Caleb taught me how to read. So I could write to you."

Papa turned and saw me standing in the doorway.

"Caleb did that?" said Papa. "All those years . . . I was so little . . . and I began to think that somehow, something I had done had made you go away."

"No," said Grandfather quickly. "What I did was wrong. Your mother and I could not live together anymore. But what I did was wrong. It was my fault. All my fault."

"Fault," said Papa very softly. "Sarah says fault doesn't matter."

Grandfather handed Papa a small sheet of paper.

"I started to write you a letter," he said.

Papa read what was written there, but didn't speak.

"It says 'I love you, Jacob,'" said Grandfather.

Papa looked at the paper for a long time.

"Don't go," he said, his voice low. "Please don't leave us again. You belong here. I don't want to miss you again. *Ever.*"

Grandfather put his arms around Papa, and they stood in the small room, holding on to each other.

I turned and went downstairs, where Sarah still sat at the kitchen table. I sat across from her.

"Remember you asked me who I wanted to be like?" I said to Sarah.

Sarah nodded.

"It's Papa. I want to be like Papa," I said.

For some reason—I couldn't say why—I began to cry. Sarah reached out and took my hand. But I cried so hard that, finally, Sarah got up and came to sit by me, putting her arms around me. Lottie and Nick came over to us, Lottie putting her head in my lap so that my tears fell onto her nose.

Cassie came into the room.

"What's wrong?" she asked.

"Nothing," said Sarah. "Not one thing in the world is wrong."

The kitchen is full of people and food. The turkey sits on the table, Grandfather carving it and cursing at it. Papa laughs at this, as if it is something old, something familiar.

Sun comes in the windows so that everything and everyone is touched by it, like gold, even Seal and Min by the fire.

Papa is smiling again. Sarah has not stopped. Even Lottie and Nick seem to smile as they hope for Grandfather to drop the turkey for them to eat.

Cassie is practicing saying a new grace, one that does not have "fuud" in it. I like the "fuud" grace myself.

Soon, Sam and Justin and Anna will drive up the road and into the yard. Everyone will run outside to greet them, and the dogs will bark and leap up, and I can tease Anna again about Justin because he is home again and safe.

Grandfather will stay. He has started writing in the journal I gave him, but he won't let me read it yet.

He says it is private.

The winter came early and will stay longer. There will be winds and storms, but I don't care. There is happiness here now. What Sarah told Cassie is true. Not one thing in the world is wrong.